**W9-BJD-416**

"I don't like to talk about my past," Jesse said.

"Me, neither." Maddie's focus rested on something beyond the laundry room. "I'm trying to concentrate on the future, on my new life."

"As a widow, you mean?" Jesse didn't quite understand why but Maddie had suddenly tensed, as if whatever was in her past was painful.

"More as a new person, an independent person who is strong enough to build a good life for herself and her son." She frowned. "I'm trying to forget my past but—sometimes it seems like there are things you'll never be able to forget. Do you know what I mean?"

"Yes." He nodded. "In a way I suppose I'm trying to do the same."

"To forget the boy you feel you failed." Maddie said it gently, as if she thought the words would hurt him, but it wasn't the words that hurt Jesse. It was knowing he'd failed Scott.

"You have such a way with my son," she said.

"He's a great kid." He felt a bubble of pleasure in having shared something so personal with Maddie.

Lois Richer loves traveling, swimming and quilting, but mostly she loves writing stories that show God's boundless love for His precious children. As she says, "His love never changes or gives up. It's always waiting for me. My stories feature imperfect characters learning that love doesn't mean attaining perfection. Love is about keeping on keeping on." You can contact Lois via email, loisricher@gmail.com, or on Facebook (loisricherauthor).

Books by Lois Richer

Love Inspired

Wranglers Ranch

The Rancher's Family Wish
Her Christmas Family Wish
The Cowboy's Easter Family Wish

Family Ties

A Dad for Her Twins
Rancher Daddy
Gift-Wrapped Family
Accidental Dad

Love For All Seasons

The Holiday Nanny
A Baby by Easter
A Family for Summer

Serenity Bay

His Winter Rose
Apple Blossom Bride
Spring Flowers, Summer Love

Visit the Author Profile page at Harlequin.com for more titles.

The Cowboy's Easter Family Wish

Lois Richer

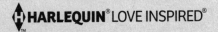
HARLEQUIN® LOVE INSPIRED®

If you purchased this book without a cover you should be aware that this book is stolen property. It was reported as "unsold and destroyed" to the publisher, and neither the author nor the publisher has received any payment for this "stripped book."

Recycling programs
for this product may
not exist in your area.

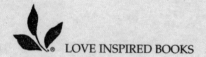

LOVE INSPIRED BOOKS

ISBN-13: 978-0-373-89921-0

The Cowboy's Easter Family Wish

Copyright © 2017 by Lois M. Richer

All rights reserved. Except for use in any review, the reproduction or utilization of this work in whole or in part in any form by any electronic, mechanical or other means, now known or hereinafter invented, including xerography, photocopying and recording, or in any information storage or retrieval system, is forbidden without the written permission of the editorial office, Love Inspired Books, 195 Broadway, New York, NY 10007 U.S.A.

This is a work of fiction. Names, characters, places and incidents are either the product of the author's imagination or are used fictitiously, and any resemblance to actual persons, living or dead, business establishments, events or locales is entirely coincidental.

This edition published by arrangement with Love Inspired Books.

® and TM are trademarks of Love Inspired Books, used under license. Trademarks indicated with ® are registered in the United States Patent and Trademark Office, the Canadian Intellectual Property Office and in other countries.

www.Harlequin.com

Printed in U.S.A.

Whatever your hands find to do,
do it with all your might.
　　　　　—*Ecclesiastes* 9:10a

Chapter One

"That's not Dad's peanut butter." Eight-year-old Noah looked shocked by his own blurted words. He quickly ducked his chin into his chest.

"We could try it." Fully aware of how much the busy Tucson grocery store aggravated her son's autism, Maddie McGregor hesitantly suggested, "You might like this kind."

"I like Dad's kind. So do twenty million other people according to ads." Noah always recited facts he'd memorized. "Dad's rule was, buy the bestseller." And he always quoted his father's rules.

Noah's hands were fluttering, a sign of his mounting agitation. Changing peanut butter brands right now wasn't worth it. Maddie set the jar back on the shelf reluctantly. She was giving in to Noah's rules. She'd vowed to stop doing that. But it had been a long day and giving in was easier than dealing with his upset behavior for the rest of the evening.

"Twenty million people could be wrong." His expression said arguing was futile. "Okay, you choose." She almost groaned when Noah selected the same oily brand his father had preferred. So much for her goal to break free of the past.

"You should give the other kind a try," a male voice suggested. "It's the one with the nut on top and if you're going to eat nut butter, you need many nuts."

"Many nuts eating nuts. Ha!" Noah's burble of laughter erupted, then died away.

Maddie turned to find a pair of twinkling blue eyes studying her from an angular sun-tanned face atop a lean, lanky cowboy. Her first thought was how carefree he looked. Her second turned to envy of his confident, relaxed stance. He looked so comfortable in his world.

When she noted a fan of tiny creases beside his eyes her envy died. He, like everyone else, no doubt had some story of past pain. She wondered half-absently what that story was before noticing the man's short cropped hair was the same shade of gold as a tropical sandy beach she'd once dreamed of visiting. And his shoulders—well, that broad width was the perfect place for a girl to rest her head.

Not *this* girl, of course, but—Maddie's cheeks burned as she visualized her late husband Liam's berating if he knew her shameful thoughts.

Forget him. You're breaking free of the past, remember?

But how to do that when her self-confidence was nil?

"I'm a peanut butter expert, ma'am." The stranger's smile coaxed her to respond to his joke. "Trust me, that brand tastes way better than the one the boy and twenty million others mistakenly prefer."

"Noah." Maddie's heart winced when her son's brown eyes flickered to the man, then skittered away, his face closing into its usual disinterested mask.

"Sorry?" The peanut butter expert arched an eyebrow.

"His name is Noah." Maddie hoped the stranger wouldn't comment on her son's now swaying body.

"Noah—like the guy with the ark," the man remarked. Something in his teasing tone caught Noah's attention, Maddie noticed. "You have lots of animals?" he continued.

"A dog. Her name is Cocoa." The swift response surprised Maddie.

"Why Cocoa?" The man looked interested, not merely polite.

"'Cause she's a chocolate lab," Noah clarified. "Dogs should be named by their features. It's not a rule but—"

"It's a good idea," the stranger finished with a nod.

"Yeah." Noah's eyes widened with surprise at his agreement.

Maddie stared at her child. Noah didn't talk or interact with strangers. Not ever.

"Chocolate labs are the best." The man thrust out his hand. "I'm Jesse Parker."

Though Noah hesitated, he couldn't ignore the gesture. His father had drummed politeness into him, one of his many unbreakable rules. Sure enough, Noah finally thrust out his small hand.

"Glad to meet, you, Noah, owner of Cocoa." Jesse's blue gaze slid to her. "And your lovely mother is?"

"Maddie McGregor." She liked the way Jesse included her.

"Maddie McGregor." He said it slowly, his forehead furrowed as if he was reaching for a stray thought. Then those blue eyes widened. "Not the amazingly talented quilter named Maddie McGregor who works for my grandmother at Quilt Essentials?"

Amazing? Talented? No one had ever called her that before.

"Grandmother—?" Maddie tried to put it together while distracted by his good looks. "Oh." Suddenly it made sense. "You're Emma's grandson."

"The best one of the bunch." He preened, then laughed. "You look shocked."

"No, I—that is, I wasn't expecting…" Thrown by his mischievous wink, Maddie gulped.

"Ninety-five percent of all children think their grandparents love them the best," said Noah, who didn't have any grandparents.

"In my case it's true." Jesse grinned.

"Emma always speaks of you as if you're four," Maddie blurted. Her cheeks burned when Jesse's hoot of amusement rippled to the ceiling. She almost checked over one shoulder before correcting the impulse.

It's been more than a year since Liam's death. He's gone. You're free now. Free.

"I guess I act that age sometimes," Jesse joked, and laughed again.

All down the grocery store aisle, heads turned to study him, and Maddie knew why. His laugh revealed the same zest for life that his grandmother possessed, the kind that beckoned you to join in. Maddie was pretty sure Jesse would be fun to be around.

Not that she was looking for fun. She was too old, too world-weary, too responsible for that kind of girlish silliness. Still, Jesse intrigued her.

"We have to go." Noah frowned at her.

Maddie studied him in confusion. Noah never volunteered conversation when strangers were present. Even more unusual, his agitated arm movements had ceased.

"What's the rush?" Jesse asked.

"Ice cream." While Noah pointed into the cart, Maddie wondered why her son was apparently unruffled when speaking to this stranger. But it didn't matter. Better to leave now, before something else upset Noah. Because something always did.

"Nice to meet you, Jesse. Thanks for the advice." In an act of defiance, she grabbed the jar of peanut butter Jesse had recommended and put it in her cart. *Baby steps to independence*, she thought defiantly.

"Uh, Maddie?" Jesse's amused voice stopped her in her tracks. She couldn't help contrasting his tone with a memory of Liam's beguiling-when-it-wanted-to-be voice that could also cut like a sword.

Immediately, her tension returned. Schooling her face into impassivity, she glanced at Jesse. "Yes?"

"I've been trying to reach my grandmother by phone with no success." His sincere friendliness chased away her tension. "I've stopped by her house a couple of times, but she doesn't answer."

"No, she wouldn't." Maddie almost groaned as Noah mumbled statistics about meeting strangers. Hopefully, Jesse hadn't noticed her discomfiture.

"Why wouldn't Gran answer?" Even Jesse's frown didn't spoil his good looks.

"She's not home." Noah's quick response surprised Maddie.

"Where is she?" Jesse glanced from him to her.

"Away." Noah's vacant stare returned, but his hands stayed by his sides, calm for now.

"Emma's at a women's retreat in the mountains of New Mexico." Maddie was puzzled by Noah's seeming tranquility. Prolonged grocery store visits usually upset him.

"She likes it there." Though Noah appeared inattentive, he was obviously keeping track of the conversation.

"Emma goes every January," Maddie clarified. "She's due back tomorrow, but you can't reach her cell because she always shuts it off for the retreat."

"I forgot about her yearly retreat." Jesse

looked so disappointed Maddie felt a twinge of pity when he added, "I wanted to surprise her, but I guess the surprise is on me."

"She's supposed to call me at work tomorrow morning." Maddie couldn't stop herself from offering to help. "Do you have a number I could give her to reach you?"

"No. I don't have a cell phone."

Maddie blinked. She'd thought Liam's refusal to own a smartphone made them virtually the only ones left behind in this age of technology. Of course, now that she was a widow she could have bought her own, but hadn't yet because of inner doubts about mastering it. Battling doubts had become an ongoing war for her mind.

"The FCC says to keep cell phones one inch from the body." Noah's speech ended as abruptly as it had begun.

"Oka-a-ay." Jesse, eyes wide, dragged out the word, then glanced at Maddie. "I let my contract expire when I left Colorado. I've been on the move for several months, so I haven't really needed a cell phone."

The way his voice tightened when he said that made her wonder if he'd left Colorado under unhappy circumstances. Funny, Emma hadn't mentioned anything.

"Well, when I see your grandmother I won't

tell her you're in town, so you can still surprise her," Maddie promised.

"Scientific studies say unexpected pleasure is more rewarding. Emma will probably like your surprise." Noah frowned at Maddie. "Ice cream?"

"Yes, we're leaving." She laid her arm protectively across his shoulders, expecting him to jerk away, and not caring. Her action was meant as a motherly defence against Jesse's searching scrutiny of her child. She hated when people gawked at Noah, then labeled him weird.

"Nice to meet you, Noah and Maddie," Jesse said.

Nice? Maddie almost laughed at the pale, insipid little word that didn't describe this encounter at all.

"Bye, Jesse." Maddie walked with Noah toward the cashier while sorting through what she'd learned about him during her three-year tenure at Quilt Essentials.

Details were scant. Though Emma constantly raved about Jesse; how loving and generous he was, how good-natured his big heart, how his love for God embraced everyone he met, the one thing she hadn't mentioned was Jesse's good looks. But then Emma was all about a person's heart, not their looks. Perhaps that's why Emma had never asked Maddie about the puckered red scar that ran from her left earlobe down her neck, the scar that made her so self-conscious.

Emma's friendship had been the lifeline Maddie had clung to—that and her own prayers that God would help her survive her marriage. Emma's quilt shop was a refuge where Maddie could bury her unhappiness in the comforting textures and glorious colors of fabrics, and let her inner soul come alive in a quilt. That very first day, Quilt Essentials had become Maddie's sanctuary and Emma the best friend she'd ever had.

Now Maddie pulled out her credit card to pay for her purchases, savoring thoughts of a relaxing evening ahead. Her hobby ranch on the outskirts of Tucson was mostly cactus and desert, but the charming, newly renovated house was all hers, the place where she could be and do what she wanted. And what Maddie wanted was to make Broken Arrow Ranch into the kind of home where Noah could enjoy a happy, carefree childhood while she taught herself to be strong and confident.

So far Maddie wasn't succeeding at either. No matter how she prayed, she couldn't shed the memory of Liam's voice constantly berating her. As for independence—well, learning to stand on your own two feet after a lifetime of having someone tell you what to do was a lot harder than she'd imagined. But she couldn't, wouldn't give up, though Noah resisted every change she tried to make.

Some days Maddie almost lost hope that she would ever feel worthy of God's love, that Noah would make friends, relax and have fun like an ordinary kid. But she didn't often pray about it anymore, because she figured Liam was right; God probably wouldn't answer the prayers of someone as unimportant as Maddie McGregor.

They were storing their groceries in the trunk of Maddie's red SUV when Noah said, "Tomorrow's Martin Luther King Day lunch. I hafta bring food to school."

"Why didn't you tell me while we were in the store?" Maddie masked her exasperation.

"Forgot." Noah shrugged. "Doesn't matter. Ninety-nine percent of the other kids will bring stuff."

"I'm sure your teacher expects one hundred percent participation." She closed the trunk with a sigh. "Come on. Let's go find something."

"You want to talk to that guy again." Noah's lecture tone reminded her of Liam. "Sometimes strangers form lasting relationships after their first meeting."

"Lasting relation—what?" Maddie gaped at him.

"Dad would be mad that you like Jesse." Noah's dark-eyed gaze met and held hers.

"Honey, your father is gone." Where did he get these statistics?

"He'd hate Jesse." Noah kicked a pebble on the pavement. "Dad never liked his kind."

"What kind?" Maddie asked. *The happy kind? The kind of person who doesn't automatically find fault?* "Jesse seems nice. And he's Emma's grandson," she reminded Noah.

"Emma's nice. But Dad wouldn't like Jesse."

"Maybe, maybe not. But that's no reason for *you* to dislike him." Maddie refused to pursue this. They both needed a break from the past. "Let's quickly get whatever you need so we can get home before the frozen stuff melts." As they walked across the lot and in through the automatic doors, she asked, "You didn't get a note from your teacher?"

"Lost it." He wouldn't look at her.

"Noah," Maddie chided, then let it go. He was always ultra responsible. Maybe losing the note was his way of avoiding the interaction of lunch. He wasn't exactly the social type. "What exactly did your teacher say?"

"Memorize six lines of Mr. King's speech and bring a food treat that will remind others of it," Noah recited in a high-pitched, singsong tone.

Maddie hid her smile. His imitation of his

teacher, Mrs. Perkins, was uncanny. "Have you memorized a portion of the speech?"

"The 'I have a dream' part." Noah's chest swelled as he precisely delivered the beginning lines of the famous speech. Then his pride visibly deflated. "I don't know any food to go with that."

"I do." Jesse stood nearby, his wonderful smile flashing. "Sorry, didn't mean to eavesdrop, but those lines always remind me of Gran's I Have a Dream snack."

"What's an I Have a Dream snack?" Noah asked, seemingly interested.

"It's pretty easy, Ark Man." Jesse grinned, and to Maddie's surprise, Noah didn't decry the nickname.

"Ark Man?" She wrinkled her nose.

"Like Noah in the Bible, Mom. 'Cause I have Cocoa. An' there's a roadrunner that goes past our place, too," he told Jesse with an eagerness she hadn't seen—maybe ever? "An' sometimes coyotes howl. An' Mom feeds hummingbirds."

"Wow." Jesse looked impressed.

"So I guess I kind of am Ark Man?" he said, obviously seeking confirmation.

"Absolutely." Jesse held up his hand to high-five, and Noah matched it. Both of them wore goofy grins.

Maddie stared at her introverted kid. This change—because of Jesse?

"So, to make these treats you need big marshmallows and some caramels," Jesse continued.

"I'll find some." Noah raced away before Maddie could stop him.

"I'm sorry. I'm interfering without even asking you," Jesse said after a quick glance at her. "I'll go get him."

"Please don't. It's the first time Noah's been that excited about anything since…ever." Without thinking, Maddie put her hand on Jesse's arm to stop him, then jerked it away when her brain repeated Noah's strangers-forming-a-relationship fact.

No relationship for her. Never going to get hurt again.

"I warn you. If this recipe of Emma's involves baking, it will be a failure."

"It will?" A puzzled look darkened his blue-eyed gaze. "But it's simple."

"Maybe, but I can't do simple baking," Maddie admitted. "Actually, I can't do complicated either," she added, eyes downcast in a rush of shame. "I'm not a good cook."

"She's not," Noah agreed solemnly, having returned with a huge bag of marshmallows. "Ninety-nine point nine percent of her cooking burns."

"Noah!" Maddie exclaimed in embarrassment.

"Fortunately, this recipe requires no cooking. Just melting." Jesse glanced at the marshmallows, then raised an eyebrow at Noah. "Caramels?"

"Couldn't find any." Noah looked dejected. "I guess we can't make the snacks."

"You can always make I Have a Dream snacks, Ark Man. One hundred percent of the time." Jesse's firm tone had the strangest effect on Noah.

"Okay." His boyish shoulders went back and his face got a determined look that Maddie had not seen before. "How?"

"We find caramels because they're the best part. And we need cream." Jesse beckoned. "Come on, you and I will check it out. They have to have them somewhere. Every self-respecting grocery store carries caramels."

"I didn't know that." Noah tucked the information away.

A bemused Maddie trailed behind the pair, accepting the pint of cream Jesse handed her as she worried about where this was going to lead. To disaster probably, and not only for Noah. Melting meant heat, which meant burning, which meant...

"Here we go. Crazy section to stock caramels in." Jesse plopped two packages into Noah's arms. "Let's make sure we've got enough for seconds."

"I'm not allowed seconds of sweets. It's a rule." The non-challenging way Noah said that made Maddie wince. What normal eight-year-old didn't automatically reach for seconds when candy was involved?

Just another thing she planned to change. Help Noah shed his stringent list of rules and become a regular kid. *Check.*

"Let's take three." She snatched another bag of caramels from the shelf. "Just in case they turn out okay."

Which they won't. She repressed the memory of that scoffing voice.

"I like your spunk, mother of Ark Man." Jesse grinned at her. "We need dry chow mein noodles, too." He laughed at their surprised expressions. "You'll see. It's delicious."

With noodles in hand, Maddie paid for their loot then led the way out of the store, wondering if sharing a sweet snack with his classmates would finally gain Noah acceptance from the other kids. He'd been an outcast for so long, mostly because of Liam's rules.

After her husband's death Maddie had blown a good part of her budget to change Noah's world. She'd located a private school that specialized in his issues and whose uniforms didn't make him look weird. She had his home hair-cut professionally restyled and enrolled him in a swimming class because he seemed to excel at that one sport. Yet despite all that, Noah still clung to his father's rules, which frustrated Maddie no end.

"Now you have everything you need, Ark Man. You and your mom can melt the caramels with a little cream, dip in the marshmallows, then roll them in the noodles. My job is done, so I'll be on my way. See you." Jesse waved and turned away.

He thought she could do this on her own?

"Wait," Maddie called out in panic. "Could you—uh, come to the house and show us exactly how to make them? Please? I'd ask Emma, but she's away."

She sounded desperate. Well, she was!

But she was asking for Noah's sake, because she wanted him to know what it was like to be the one to bring a special treat, to be in the limelight in a good way. Just once she wanted Noah to be envied by other kids instead of being mocked.

And maybe you're asking because you like the way Jesse didn't make fun of you for not being able to cook.

Her son frowned in confusion. "Mom?" he whispered. "Stranger rule?"

Liam's rules had taught Noah fear, and Maddie saw it now in his brown eyes. She was usually wary of strangers, too. But funnily enough, not with Jesse.

Why was that?

"Um, maybe I shouldn't go to your place," Jesse said, his gaze on Noah. "I could just—"

"Please come," she invited, discounting her inhibitions. "I'd really like to make this treat."

"I guess, if you're sure?" After a moment's pause Jesse added, "Since Gran's away I haven't got anything special on tonight. Maybe after we're finished I could use your phone to call Wranglers Ranch about a job?"

"Sure. Tanner Johns owns Wranglers. His wife, Sophie, is a friend of mine. Actually, we're neighbors." Maddie stashed the second set of groceries in her vehicle. "If you help us, I'll put in a good word for you in exchange."

Maybe she wasn't being totally straightforward by not telling Jesse that his grandmother was an ardent supporter of Wranglers Ranch and its outreach mission for troubled kids, or that Emma's referral would probably be far more valuable than hers. But Maddie needed Jesse's help. For Noah. So she waited on pins and needles.

"Okay, it's a deal." Jesse motioned to a battered brown half-ton truck that sat at the far end of the parking lot. "That's mine. How far is your place?"

"About ten minutes outside the city. We live on Broken Arrow Ranch. You can follow us there." Maddie waited with bated breath until he nodded. As he walked away she was surprised to see him clap a black Stetson on his head. Where had that come from?

You were too busy gawking at his hunky face to notice his hat.

"I guess Jesse's nice. But Dad's rule..." Noah's confused voice died away.

"Jesse is Emma's grandson. He's like a friend." She was doing this for Noah. She'd do anything to help him.

You're making another mistake, Madelyn.

That voice killed the confidence she'd had in her hasty invitation, until she remembered her last talk with her boss.

Maddie, you went from being a child to being a wife and then a mom. Now you need to take the time to figure out who Maddie is. Not Maddie, Liam's wife, or Maddie, Noah's Mom, but Maddie, the beloved child of God. The first step is to learn to trust your Heavenly Father.

Okay then. She'd take this step, and maybe if she trusted God enough, He'd show her the next one, the step that would help Noah heal.

"Jesse calls me Ark Man," Noah mused aloud.

"Is that okay?" she asked.

"I guess." A tiny smile curved his lips. "I never had a nickname before."

Because Liam hadn't allowed them.

"It makes you feel kind of special," Noah said thoughtfully.

Maddie pulled into her yard with a sense of wonder. Because of Jesse, her son the rule-keeper was changing. Was this the beginning of the breakthrough she'd been praying for?

What else could happen?

Jesse was simply going to show Maddie and her kid how to make the treats his gran had taught him to make when he was Noah's age.

He was *not* going to get involved. So what could happen?

As he climbed out of his truck his stomach issued a loud and angry protest at its empty state. He stomped his boots free of the dust to cover the rumblings. He'd been counting on one of Gran's delicious meals to satiate his hunger. Clearly, that wasn't going to happen, but maybe Maddie wouldn't mind if he gobbled up a few of her treats.

Jesse could tell by the look on the kid's face when Maddie invited him inside that Noah minded him being there. Obviously, he'd heard many warnings to be careful of strangers. Not a bad thing, Jesse decided.

"This is a beautiful spread." He glanced around appreciatively. "The untouched desert is fascinating."

"I think so, too." Maddie looked surprised by his comment. "I often sit on the porch with my coffee in the morning and just enjoy it. I love the peace."

Meaning she hadn't had a lot of peace in her life? Curiosity about this woman mushroomed as Jesse took the grocery bags from her.

"The mountains make a great backdrop," Maddie said, as she unlocked the door and pushed it open. "Although coming from Colorado, you probably think ours are puny."

"No such—oof." Jesse struggled to keep his balance as a chocolate lab jumped up at him. "Pleased to meet you, Cocoa." He chuckled as the dog licked his hands.

"Oh, I'm so sorry. Down, Cocoa." Maddie tugged at the animal's collar, dragging the dog away from Jesse. "Take her outside, Noah."

Jesse noted the boy's frown as his glance moved from her face to his, his eyes dark and stormy.

"Now, please, son," Maddie said.

After a moment Noah nodded and clipped the lead on the dog's collar.

"Hang on tight, Ark Man," Jesse advised, as he plopped the grocery bags on the counter. "That's a strong animal you're taking out of the ark."

Noah almost cracked a smile as he half walked, half dragged Cocoa outside.

"She's a bit of a handful for him, but I'm hoping they'll soon get used to each other." Maddie smiled at Jesse's questioning look. "Cocoa was my Christmas gift to Noah."

"Nice gift." *Her* Christmas gift, not *our* gift, he noted. So where was the kid's father?

"If you want to wash before we make the treats, the bathroom's just down the hall," Maddie offered.

"Thanks." Jesse walked past her, noticing that aside from the caramels and marshmallows, there were no frivolous purchases. Fruit, vegetables, bread, frozen dinners, peanut butter and milk. The basics. No cookies, no chips, no junk food at all, except for the caramels and marshmallows. Poor Noah.

She pressed the answering machine and listened to Noah's teacher while she unpacked and stored her groceries.

Jesse took his time scrubbing up. When he returned to the kitchen, Maddie was telling Noah to leave the dog outdoors. On the deck outside, Cocoa was busy chowing down. Every so often she gave a guttural woof, glanced around, then returned to eating.

"Cocoa likes it better out there than inside the ark."

Jesse did a double take. Noah's face looked blank, but a tiny smile twitched at the corner of his lips. He chuckled. The stiff-necked kid had actually made a joke.

"So how do we make these treats?" With an apron wrapped around her narrow waist, Maddie stood primly poised behind the breakfast bar, hands folded, waiting for directions.

Jesse got trapped admiring the way her chin-length black hair glistened like an ebony frame around her oval face with its huge green eyes. Her lashes, long and lush, helped accentuate the smooth angles and curves of her sculpted cheeks, complimented by a pert nose and full lips. Maddie wasn't tall, yet when Noah was near she somehow seemed stronger, invincible.

Jesse also glimpsed in Noah's mother an innocence, a delicate fragility. For as long as he could remember he'd had this weird ability to see beneath the mask others presented. That proficiency now told him that Maddie had suffered, but somehow Jesse knew that though bent like a reed in the wind, she had not been broken by her suffering. Instead, the tentative way she smiled at him added to his hunch that hardship had left Maddie McGregor stronger, still genuine and sincere, uncorrupted.

Exactly the opposite of his own world-weariness.

"Is something wrong, Jesse?" Her considerate tone pulled him back from the cliff of his sad memories.

Who *was* Maddie McGregor?

"I shouldn't have pushed you to do this tonight. You've been traveling." She offered him a sympathetic smile. "I'm sure you're tired. Maybe it would be better—"

"I'm fine." He noticed Noah sitting on the other side of the breakfast bar, watching them with those dark see-all eyes. "Gonna help, Ark Man? It's for your class, isn't it?"

Silent, Noah slid off his stool and joined his mother.

"First we need a heavy saucepan half full of water," Jesse explained. "Once the water's hot we can set another smaller pan inside it to melt the caramels."

Without a word, Maddie produced a pair of saucepans, half-filled the larger one with water and set it to heat on the expansive gas range.

"Okay?" she asked, a nervous edge to her voice.

"Great." Jesse smiled to reassure her. "Let's

start unwrapping those caramels and putting them in this smaller pan."

"How many?" Noah deftly slid a candy out of its covering, but made no attempt to eat it.

"How many kids in your class?" Jesse hid his surprise when Noah said eleven. "Small class."

"He attends a private school," Maddie explained.

"Okay, so eleven kids, multiplied by at least three treats for each. Let's make fifty." Jesse grinned at their surprise. "One of these is never enough, you'll see. Plus they are small. Oh. I forgot to ask if you have toothpicks." He noticed Maddie's forehead crease in a frown. "Something we could use as skewers?" he prodded.

"I don't think so," she murmured.

"Does that mean we can't make them?" Noah looked worried.

"We can still make them, but it's much easier if we have something we can poke through the marshmallow to dip into the melted caramels, and leave in so we can stand it up." Jesse wasn't sure why, but suddenly it seemed very important that he help this woman and her child make his gran's treat. "I could run back into town—"

"Dad got sticks for my science project. There were some left." Noah's eagerness made Jesse smile.

"Honey, I have no idea where those might

be." Maddie's cheeks grew pink. She did not look at her son. "When we moved here we had so much stuff and—"

"And you wanted to get rid of Dad's stuff," Noah's harsh voice accused. "Waste not, want not. That was his rule."

"Yes, it was." Maddie's voice dropped to a whisper.

Jesse hated the way her lovely face closed up, like a daisy when the sun went behind a cloud. He had to do something.

"Can you call your dad and ask him if he knows where they might be?" he suggested.

The room went utterly still.

"He's dead." Noah's voice broke. He glared at his mother. "You hated his rules, but I don't." Then he raced from the room.

Jesse had vowed not to get personally involved in a kid's life again, not after the fiasco in Colorado. Why hadn't he stayed out of his grandmother's favorite grocery store tonight? Why hadn't he avoided this woman and her troubled kid, simply swallowed his impulse to help?

Most of all, what was he supposed to do now to stem the tears tumbling down Maddie's white cheeks as she stared after Noah?

Lord, You know how I've failed others. You

know I've vowed not to get involved again, to never again risk failing a child.

So, God, what am I doing here with this woman and her troubled son?

Chapter Two

Weeping in front of a stranger?

Liam would—*Forget him!*

"I'm sorry." Maddie swiped a hand across her wet face. "Noah is still struggling to deal with his father's death."

"How long has it been?" Jesse asked quietly.

For the first time since she'd met him, Maddie tried to recall Emma's words about her grandson. Why had he offered to help them, strangers he didn't even know?

"Liam died of a heart attack just over a year ago."

"A heart attack?"

She saw Jesse's eyes flare with surprise and felt compelled to explain. "I'm twenty-seven. Liam was eighteen years older than me."

"His death must have been very hard on both

you and Noah," Jesse said in the gentlest tone. "So after he died, you moved here?"

"We were renting a house that belonged to the church Liam pastored. We had to move because they needed the house for their new minister." Maddie wasn't about to admit just how eagerly she'd left that unhappy place. "Noah and I rented for a while, then moved to Broken Arrow Ranch last summer."

"I see." Jesse nodded. "That's a lot of change for any kid to handle."

She immediately bristled, then realized Jesse wasn't criticizing, simply stating facts. And yet she still asked, "Do you think I was wrong to move here?"

"Are you kidding?" Jesse chuckled. "It was dusk when we drove up, so I didn't get the full impact, but what I did glimpse of your spread was impressive. I doubt anyone would fault you for wanting to live here."

"I love it," she whispered, but she didn't tell him it was because the ranch represented freedom. Maddie glanced out the window as she explained the rest of her story. "Broken Arrow belonged to an elderly couple. They'd just completed interior renovations when the husband got sick. When they decided to move closer to medical care, Emma and Tanner both suggested I buy this place."

"Tanner—of Wranglers Ranch?" Jesse interjected.

"Yes. I think he and Sophie wanted to make sure they got a good neighbor. They helped us move here. But I'm not sure they've benefited much. I've had to call Tanner for help with a mouse—twice." Maddie chuckled. "The upside for us is that Sophie's a caterer. She often invites us over to try her new recipes and they are always delicious. I think I got the better deal when it comes to neighbors."

"Ah." His eyes twinkled with fun. "They get a good neighbor and you get good food. You're a smart lady."

"Not that smart." Maddie frowned. "What do we do for skewers?"

"Why is making this so important to you?" Jesse asked curiously. "It's just candy."

She glanced at the doorway through which her son had disappeared a few moments earlier, then answered in a hushed tone. "It's not just candy to me. It's a chance for Noah."

"To do what?" Jesse scanned the caramels and marshmallows. "This isn't the stuff heroes are made of."

"It could be." Maddie wasn't above begging when it was for Noah. "Please, Jesse, show us how to make these treats."

She held her breath. Emma said Maddie was

God's child. Surely He would help her convince Jesse to help them?

Jesse had never been able to turn down anyone who asked him for help, and despite his recent vow to remain uninvolved, he couldn't do it this time, either. Calling himself an idiot, he began unwrapping more candy, adding to the contents in the saucepan, which he noted was gleaming and without a scratch.

She was a mom with a kid of, what? Seven? Eight? But apparently she'd barely used these like-new saucepans.

Jesse glanced around. Come to think of it, the furniture looked brand-new, too. Nicely tailored, not fussy, definitely comfortable, with quilts scattered here and there. Precise, finely patterned quilts with detailed stitching... Everything looked unused.

Also, everything was in its place. There wasn't a speck of dust or a mess anywhere, no toy tossed here or a shirt discarded there. To Jesse, eldest of four rambunctious kids, this didn't look like the home of a dog and a young boy. It was too—*restrained*. As if it hadn't yet become home.

Two pictures hung on the wall. One was a very large portrait of Noah staring at a birthday cake with eight burning candles. The second was a smaller photo of him and Maddie standing by a flowering cactus. There were no snapshots or precious photos of the late husband and father. Questions multiplied inside Jesse's head.

"What can we substitute for the skewers?" Maddie asked, drawing him from his introspection.

"Forks, I guess. You don't have regular toothpicks? Because they would work," he said, as he added a small dollop of cream to the melting candy.

"No, I'm pretty sure I don't—oh, wait." With a smile as big as Texas Maddie flung open a cabinet and lifted out a massive cellophane-covered basket. "This was a housewarming gift from your grandmother. I guess she thought we'd be camping out or something, because she put in a bunch of disposable things. Maybe there's something we could use in here."

She pawed her way through the crackling cellophane, pulling out items and discarding them on the stone countertop in her search for toothpicks.

"Well?" Jesse waited, content to watch this beautiful woman.

"Nothing." Maddie's tone deflated when she came to the bottom of the basket.

"These might work." He selected and rotated a box.

"What are they?" She leaned across him to read the label. "Oh. Stir sticks." She turned away, then stopped and turned back, eyes glowing as she took the package and tore it open. "Stir sticks!" she repeated, her grin wide as she held up a handful.

"Wooden ones, which are perfect, though I'm surprised my tasteful grandmother chose such lurid colors." He plunged the tip of one purple-and-green-striped stick into a marshmallow and grinned right back at her. "Hey, Ark Man," he called. "We're making the treats. You better come help us so you'll be able to tell the other kids how to make 'em."

Jesse hadn't given a thought to calling Noah until he glanced at Maddie and suddenly realized he should have let her do that. He opened his mouth to apologize, but she stopped him with a tearful look.

"Thank you," she whispered, just before her son appeared. "We found stir sticks for the I Have a Dream treats, Noah. Emma sent them in that basket of stuff."

"Huh." Noah watched Jesse, who drew his attention to the melting caramels. The boy spread the crisp noodles on a sheet of wax paper as directed, then mimicked Jesse's action, dipping a skewered marshmallow into the melted candy, rolling it in the noodles and standing it in a glass to set.

"Wait," Jesse ordered, when they'd made a total of three treats. Mother and son turned questioning gazes on him. "There's no point in making any more unless they taste okay. Go ahead," he urged Noah. "Do a taste test."

Noah glanced at his mom, who nodded. With exaggerated slowness he lifted one of the sticks from the glass and tried to bite the caramel. Of course the marshmallow moved, escaping his teeth. Jesse couldn't control his amusement, until Noah set the stick down, his face a wounded mask.

"This is what you looked like." Jesse made a fool of himself trying to coax a laugh from Noah and his mother and finally succeeded. "Now this is the proper way to eat them, or at least it's how I've always eaten them." He popped an entire marshmallow into his mouth, closed his eyes and chewed. "Mmm. I'd forgotten how good these were." He savored the taste.

Maddie reached for the last one. She put it in her mouth hesitantly, but then her eyes widened as she chewed.

"Noah," she said, wonder coloring her musical voice. "Taste it. They're delicious."

"Sweets are bad for you," Noah recited. "A

third of all children starting school have tooth decay."

"It's okay to have a treat now and then," she told him.

Jesse could see how hard the boy was finding it to taste the candy. Those rules again. Someone had sure brainwashed him.

"Too many sweets are bad for you," he agreed. "But you're not going to have too many. Are you, Ark Man?"

After a moment, Noah shook his head, picked up his skewer and studied it with a critical eye. "I like triangles," he said firmly. "They're the best. These are circles."

Jesse blinked. "Uh, I don't know how to make them into triangles."

"It doesn't matter." Maddie intervened with a smile. "Just try it, Noah," she encouraged. "Circles are good, too. Think about apples and oranges."

"I like triangles." But he did slide the covered marshmallow into his mouth. The myriad of expressions that chased across his face was a delight Jesse was glad he was there to witness.

"So tell me, Ark Man, are circles okay?"

Still chewing, Noah nodded vigorously.

"And do you think three each will be enough for your classmates?"

He shook his head in a very firm no.

"Then let's get busy," Jesse urged.

They worked together in a relay. With delicate precision Noah speared the marshmallows, then handed the skewers to Jesse for dipping. He passed them on to Maddie to roll in the noodles. Halfway through they changed positions, so Maddie could dip and Noah could roll. And somewhere in the midst of the laughing and giggling and sneaky licks of a finger, Noah became an ordinary kid making a treat in the kitchen.

When Jesse glanced at Maddie he found her watching him, appreciation shining from the depths of her gorgeous green eyes. He couldn't look away, but she did, quickly, as if she was embarrassed.

"We've used all the marshmallows, so I guess it's time to clean up, and you need to get ready for bed." Maddie mussed Noah's too-perfect hair and pressed a kiss on his head. "How shall we keep these overnight, Jesse?"

"Just leave them. They'll dry out and firm up a bit. Then you can lay them in a box or container for school tomorrow." He was embarrassed by his stomach's loud rumble.

"Didn't you eat dinner?" Noah paused in his cleanup of the leftover noodle bits.

"I didn't." Jesse shrugged. "That's why I went to the grocery store. It's Gran's favorite. When she wasn't at home, I hoped I'd find her there and that maybe she'd have dinner with me when she was finished shopping. Or maybe make me dinner." He shook his head. "Doesn't matter. I'll get something to eat on my way back to my campsite."

"You're camping?" Noah's bored look vanished, replaced by excitement.

"Ever since I left Colorado, Ark Man."

"In a tent? With a campfire? And cookouts?" Awe filled Noah's voice.

"All of the above," Jesse agreed.

"Cool." The word whooshed out of Noah as if he could only imagine such a life.

"It is fun, except when it rains or there are mosquitos. Thankfully, the desert has little of either right now." Jesse turned to Maddie. "I've taken some time away from work to see this country," he explained.

"What is your work?" she asked.

"I'm—I was a youth pastor." He could almost feel her draw back when he said the word *pastor*. "I, ah, needed a break."

"I see." Maddie's face tightened into a mask. She abruptly turned her focus on Noah. "Get ready for bed, please."

"Eight o'clock is bedtime," Noah explained with a sigh. "It's the rule." He hesitated. "Will I see you again, Jesse?"

"I hope so, Ark Man. I intend to apply for a job at Wranglers Ranch. That's right next door, your mom says." He smiled at the boy, but Noah was deep in thought.

"You're a minister," he said quietly, then glanced up. "Like my dad was?"

"Not anymore." Jesse felt funny saying that, as if God had somehow rescinded the call He'd made on his life so many years ago. "For now I'm going to try being a ranch hand." *Until I figure out what God's doing and what I'm supposed to do.*

"My dad said that when you work for God you can't quit," Noah said firmly. "He said that God wouldn't let him quit. He said it was a pastor's rule."

"For him, sweetie. It was a rule for *him*." Maddie nudged his thin shoulder. "Now thank Jesse for showing us how to make the treats."

Noah obediently thanked him, but it was clear that though he left without further protest, the question of Jesse's unemployment was not settled.

"I should get going, too," he said.

"Please stay and share a cup of tea, maybe a sandwich?" Maddie stood at the counter, hands knotted as if she was nervous. Her black cap of hair gleamed under the lights. "I'm no cook, but I owe you at least that much."

"You don't owe me anything. But I wouldn't say no to a cup of tea. Or a sandwich," he added, when his stomach complained again.

"I can do a sandwich." Maddie's face looked like the sun had come out, so brilliant was her smile. She put the kettle on, then pulled open the fridge. "What would you like?"

"Anything is fine. Thank you." He hoped she'd offer a thick slice of roast beef with hot mustard on fresh French bread. Or maybe—

"Is peanut butter okay?" Maddie stood in front of her fridge, clutching an almost empty jar of peanut butter, the same wimpy brand Noah preferred. "I could mix it with honey," she offered.

"Great." Jesse sat at the counter and accepted the sandwich when she served it, biting into it with relish, smiling and nodding as he chewed. "It's good."

"I should have made you something nice. I wish I could. You deserve it." She sat one stool away from him, elbows propped on the counter, inhaling the steam from her tea. "Here I have this designer kitchen that most women dream of, and I'm a useless cook."

That sounded like something someone had called her.

"Why don't you take cooking lessons?" he

asked, after swallowing the sticky mass. "Gran made my mom take them."

"Really?" Maddie looked as if she'd never heard of such a thing.

"Sure. When my parents lived here there was a cooking school called Alberto's Mama. That's where my mom went to learn to cook before she had me." He grinned. "Gran insisted it was a necessity and my dad was happy to pay when he started tasting Alberto's Mama's recipes. Was your husband a cook?" He pretended to ask out of idle curiosity.

Immediately, Maddie went tense. Her fingers tightened around her cup and her cheeks lost the delightful pink that had bloomed there. "Gourmet," she murmured.

And that only made you feel worse.

Jesse's heart hurt at the wounded look on her face. "I'm sure you have talents in other areas."

She laughed, head thrown back, throat bare. It was the way Maddie should always laugh— full-bodied and freely expressing her emotions, Jesse thought. Not like that timid, fearful mouse he'd glimpsed a few moments ago.

"I don't have many talents, but I can make a pretty good quilt," she agreed with a cheeky grin, then quickly sobered. "Though some say that's a pointless and dying art."

"Since when is giving comfort pointless?"

Jesse was angry that someone had so cruelly disparaged her gift. "When I was a kid I used to go with Gran to take her quilts to the cancer ward and to the homeless shelters. People loved her gifts because the quilts made them feel special and cherished, as if they mattered. That feeling is an amazing gift to give someone. It takes real talent. Cooking is just following directions."

Jesse hadn't meant to sound off, but when he noticed Maddie's spine straighten he was glad he had, now certain of his original assessment that someone hadn't properly valued this woman. He got caught up in speculating who that was, but his thoughts were interrupted by a call from the bedroom.

"Excuse me." Maddie disappeared into Noah's room with a smile, but when she emerged moments later her green eyes swirled with uneasiness.

"Everything okay with the Ark Man?" he asked.

"Noah's fine." Maddie frowned. "Why do you call him that?"

"Ark Man?" He shrugged. "Noah seems all about formalism, rules, that kind of thing. I've found—I used to find," he corrected, "—that sometimes a nickname helps break through the mask most overly responsible kids wear. I can stop if you want."

"Please don't." There was something about Maddie now—a tightness that echoed the tension on her pretty face. "Noah likes that nickname."

Jesse couldn't define the vibe he was getting, but that openness he'd so admired about her earlier had disappeared. He had the impression it had to do with him having been a minister—like her husband.

"Noah would like to speak to you for a minute."

"Sure." He walked toward the room Maddie indicated, and stepped inside, surprised by the plain simplicity of it. No superhero posters, no toys scattered around, no video games or computer. No distractions. Just one small bedside photo of a man with dark hair graying at the temples and a severe-looking face. Noah's father, Jesse guessed. "Hey. Ready for bed, huh?"

"Yes." Noah lay tucked in his bed, covered to his chin in a gorgeous gray quilt with puffy, silver-white clouds delicately dotting the surface. Somehow Jesse knew Maddie had made it. "Thank you for helping my mom and me make the treats, Jesse."

"You're very welcome. I hope you enjoy them." Jesse could tell the boy wanted to ask something, so even though Maddie stood behind him, ready to escort him out, he waited.

"Sometime…" Noah paused, glanced at his mother, then let the words spill out. "If it's not too much trouble, could you maybe show me your tent and campfire and—everything?"

"Sure." There was such a longing in the boy's request that Jesse couldn't let it be. "We'll make s'mores," he promised.

"Some mores?" Noah frowned. "What's that?"

"S'mores." He grinned. "Did you like the I Have a Dream snacks?"

"Oh, yes." Noah licked his lips with relish.

"Then you'll like s'mores," Jesse promised with a chuckle. "After I talk to the people at Wranglers and find out if I can get a job, I'll check with your mom and we'll set up a time for you to visit my campsite. Okay?"

"Thank you very much." Noah's eyes shone.

"You're welcome. Good night, Ark Man."

"Good night, PBX." A sly smile lit his face.

"Pardon?" Jesse couldn't figure out what the letters meant, but the boy wore a smug look. "What's a PBX?"

"Peanut butter expert." Noah grinned when Jesse laughed. Then he suddenly looked worried. "Is it okay?"

"It's an excellent nickname. Thank you, Ark Man. Sleep well."

Noah nodded, snuggled his head against the pillow and closed his eyes.

Jesse followed Maddie to the living room and sat in the chair she indicated, still chuckling.

"PBX. What a kid." He caught her studying him. "By the way, if his quilt is an example of what you can create with mere fabric," he said, "I'm in awe. Forget learning to cook. Your work is spectacular."

"Thank you." She actually blushed at the compliment. "It couldn't be bright and colorful, so I did the next best thing. Noah seems to like it."

"Why couldn't it be bright?" Jesse was curious about her response. "Are colors against Noah's rules?"

"No." She gave him a quick glance, then shifted her gaze to somewhere beyond his shoulder. "Noah is autistic. Too many bright colors or vivid patterns create heightened stimulation and that stresses him. So I tried to make his room calm but still attractive, a place where he can rest, concentrate, be at peace."

"Looks to me like you succeeded. With him, too. He's a great kid."

"Thank you." Maddie twiddled her fingers together, then looked directly at him. "I guess you know a lot about kids, having been a youth pastor."

"I don't know as much as I should," Jesse said bitterly, his joy in Noah's excitement evaporating. If he was going to hang with her son, Maddie deserved to know the truth. "One of the kids in my group committed suicide and I'm to blame."

"Why?" Her soft question wasn't perfunctory. She leaned forward, her eyes wide with interest, as she waited for his response.

"Because I couldn't stop him." How it hurt to admit that.

"I don't understand." Maddie frowned. "Were you there at the time?"

"No. Scott was at home, in his room, when he took an overdose of pills." Jesse gave the details clearly and concisely, his guilt burgeoning with each word. "His parents found him in the morning, lifelessly clutching a note that said he was being bullied and wanted to make it stop." Waves of self-recrimination returned.

"Oh, no." Her whisper of empathy helped him continue.

"I was Scott's friend as well as his youth pastor. I saw him at least three times a week. I took him for a soda that very afternoon." He shook his head. "Why didn't I know? Why didn't I see something?"

"I'm so sorry, Jesse." Maddie's sympathy brought him back to the present.

"Thanks. I had to tell you."

"You did?" Her green gaze widened. "Why?"

"In case you don't want me to be around Noah." To his utter shock and dismay, Maddie began to laugh. "What's so funny?"

"You." She shook her head. "Jesse, do you have any idea how I've longed for my son to break free of his autism long enough to find joy in kid things?"

He shook his head.

"Only since he was diagnosed, when he was three," she told him, her tone fierce. "Tonight, for the first time in eons, I watched Noah become engaged and interested, really interested, in something."

"It was just candy."

"*Just* candy?" Maddie chuckled. "Noah doesn't eat candy. Ever. He only talks about candy, repeatedly reciting his father's rule about its unhealthiness. Tonight, somehow, you got him to not only make candy but eat it *and* enjoy it. That's huge."

"I'm glad if he did." Jesse grinned. "Even if it wasn't triangles."

"He has a thing about triangles. But that isn't all you did." Maddie's lashes were suddenly wet as a tear rolled down her cheek. When she looked at him, deep love for her precious boy lay vulnerably revealed. "You talked to him, not at him. You treated him as if he's normal kid."

"Well, he is. Isn't he?" Jesse frowned at her.

"Noah has…issues other kids don't have. He's very reclusive. He doesn't interact easily and yet tonight you discovered interests in him that I never even imagined. Nicknames. Camping." She shook her head, a rueful look on her face. "How could I not have known Noah was interested in camping? Liam was right. Sometimes I am just plain dumb."

"Liam being…?" Jesse had to ask, though he was pretty sure he already knew who this denigrating person was.

"Liam was my husband. That's his picture by Noah's bed." A rueful smile lifted the edges of her lips. "You probably wonder how I could have married a man so much older than me."

That question along with a hundred more about this amazing woman had burned through his brain, but Jesse remained silent, letting her speak on her own terms.

"Everyone wants to know that and the answer is…" she paused, her face tightening "…escape. You told me about your past, so I'll share some of mine." She took a deep breath. "My father was abusive when he got drunk. I spent my childhood and youth avoiding him, hiding out at a friend's, keeping his secret, trying to finish my studies so I could graduate and leave."

"But you should have—"

"Told someone?" A half smile that held no mirth lifted her lips. "I did once and paid for it dearly. I knew that if I told again, I would only get hurt that much more. I wasn't that stupid," she added, almost defiantly.

"So Liam came along," Jesse murmured, knowing exactly where this was going.

"He stopped by initially to invite my father to his church, and then he just kept coming back. I could tell he was interested in me, but I never took it seriously. I didn't know anything about men. I was so naive." She looked embarrassed and…ashamed? "One day my dad came home in a foul mood. He'd lost his job and he was drunk. Very drunk. And I was his punching bag."

Anger burned inside Jesse for the girl she'd been, alone, unprotected and unloved. But he held his tongue, letting her vent, because he'd learned the abused often needed to verbalize their pain.

"I endured as long as I could, but later, when he zonked out, I saw my chance and I ran away. I was huddled on a park bench when Liam found me. He bought me some new clothes to replace my torn ones, fed me and then he proposed."

Again that unamused smile. "He was my way out and I grabbed at the chance."

"That was the night you got the scar." Jesse didn't need to see her nod or the way she lifted her hand to touch the puckered skin to know the truth. "I don't blame you for seizing the opportunity."

He hesitated. He'd vowed not to get personally involved again, but he couldn't just up and leave her like this, stuck in what sounded like a miserable past.

"It wasn't a good marriage," Maddie whispered, her voice forlorn. "I didn't know anything about being a wife, let alone a pastor's wife. I couldn't cook and the child I bore was what Liam called defective. My fault. I was a failure."

"How could Noah's autism possibly be your fault?" Jesse demanded. "And he is *not* defective," he hissed through clenched teeth.

"Thank you for saying that." She offered him the saddest of smiles. "To be fair, my husband was much older and not used to children. Noah had colic. He cried a lot and that got on Liam's nerves. I guess that's why he stopped asking me to be involved in the church, and left me to tend our son. As Noah got older and other problems emerged, Liam decided the way to control

Noah's outbursts was to instill in him a set of unbreakable rules."

"Ah," Jesse said, understanding. "Noah learned he could please his father if he obeyed all the rules."

"Exactly." Maddie grew thoughtful. "I'm not exactly sure why, but now Liam's gone and Noah still clings to those rules, even though his dad is no longer here to approve. I'm trying to break his reliance on them by showing him that rules are only a guide."

"And that maybe some of those rules are wrong?" Jesse added very quietly.

"Yes." She lifted her head and thrust out her chin. "That's why what you did for him tonight is so amazing. Jesse, I have never seen Noah so eager about anything. I'd really appreciate it if you could take him to see your campsite. I don't want to inconvenience you, but if he's truly interested in camping, perhaps I can find a way to build on that."

"I don't know exactly how long I'll be in Tucson." Jesse was cautious, aware that it would be all too easy to get involved with this pretty mom and her needy child. "But I'll certainly show him my campsite and cook him some s'mores, as I promised."

"Thank you. I appreciate it." She grinned cheekily. "Emma was right about you. You really are something." Then she sobered. "May I speak plainly?"

"Of course." He wondered what was coming.

"I want—in fact, I crave—your help with Noah. But I don't want there to be any mistakes between us to spoil things."

"Okay." Where was this going?

"Please be clear that I am not looking for anything more, Jesse."

"Pardon?" He watched her face flush and her hands knot as she said it, but Maddie's intense gaze held his.

"I'm not looking for a husband or a father for my son. I was not a good wife. I did not love my husband the right way. I was a failure and one mistake was more than enough." Maddie paused, then offered, "I'm not interested in romance. But I surely could use a friend."

"You've got one." Relieved, Jesse relaxed. "I feel the same. My fiancée recently dumped me. It's been painful to discover that the woman I thought I'd love forever was not the person I believed her to be, and that I wasn't the one she really wanted. She preferred my best friend. I still feel stupid, and I sure don't want to go through that again, you know?"

He gulped, then expelled a rush of relief when Maddie nodded in understanding.

"I don't think I'm meant to be anyone's mate."

Jesse figured he might as well be blunt. "But friendship is something I think we could share. To help Noah." He held out his hand. "So hello, friend Maddie."

"Hello, friend Jesse." Her slim fingers slid into his and gripped with a firmness he hadn't expected. "Whatever I can help *you* with, just ask."

"A recommendation to Wranglers Ranch?" he suggested, as he drew his hand away, surprised that the warmth of her gentle touch lingered on his skin.

Maddie smiled, picked up the phone and dialed.

"Tanner, this is Maddie. We're good, thanks. How's baby Carter?" She chuckled at the response. "Poor you. Call me to babysit anytime. Listen, Tanner, I have a friend who's looking for a job. I think he'd be perfect for Wranglers Ranch. His name is Jesse. He's Emma's grandson... Okay, I will. Bye." She ended the call. "Stop by Wranglers anytime tomorrow."

Jesse's jaw dropped. "Just like that?"

"I told you there were advantages to living next door to Tanner and Sophie."

"Thank you," he said, and he meant it.

"You're welcome." When she checked her watch Jesse took that as his cue to leave.

"I should go. Thank you for a fun evening,

Maddie. I enjoyed myself." He rose and walked to the door, aware of her slight figure padding barefoot behind him. He pushed open the screen door and caught his breath.

The desert beyond lay in darkness save for an array of solar lights.

"It looks like someone painted a giant stained-glass butterfly." He turned to look at her. "You?"

Maddie nodded, a satisfied smile tipping up her rosy lips.

"How?" Jesse couldn't imagine the hours it must have taken to place each lamp just so in order to create this intricate design.

"I used a quilt pattern. Noah helped me get the wings right." Her green eyes peered into the distance but Jesse was fairly certain she wasn't staring at the lights because after a moment she said in a whisper-soft voice, "I dreamed of creating it a long time ago." Her gaze slid to study him. "Maybe this is the year for my dreams to come true. First we moved to my ranch, then my butterfly became reality and now you're here helping Noah."

My ranch. *My* butterfly. Something about the way she said it got Jesse pondering what other dreams this woman held tucked deep inside.

"Will you be able to find your way to your campsite from here?"

Maddie looked so concerned that he hurried to remind her that he and his parents had once lived in Tucson.

"I'm glad you came back, Jesse."

"So am I." He walked toward his truck and was about to climb in when her quiet call stopped him.

"Jesse?"

"Yes?" He paused and peered toward her slim figure, saw her hands grip the balustrade as she tilted forward.

"Thank you very much." The soft words brimmed with intensity.

He waved, then got into his truck and drove away, wondering why he knew that quiet expression of gratitude came from her heart.

Maddie McGregor was a puzzle. She seemed young and innocent, and yet was apparently the product of a miserable childhood and a wretched marriage. Gutsy but somehow vulnerable. Nightshade and sunshine. She had a home taken straight from the pages of a magazine, but apart from a couple of quilts tossed over the sofa, it looked too neat to be truly lived in. In fact, aside from her quilts, there wasn't much in that house that said anything about Maddie McGregor.

That whimsical butterfly, however, said a lot. And that intrigued him.

When Gran came home Jesse intended to spend an evening plying her with questions about his new friend.

But as he lay in his tent, he had to remind himself to stop thinking about sweet Maddie McGregor.

You can't get involved. Nobody else gets hurt, remember?

Chapter Three

"Jesse." Tanner Johns shook his hand heartily. "You're Maddie's friend."

Relief suffused Jesse. After the fiasco in his Colorado church there hadn't been many who'd wanted to call him friend.

"And you're Emma's grandson." Tanner grinned. "Welcome to Wranglers Ranch."

"Thanks." A little taken aback by the warmth of his greeting, Jesse figured the cowboy must not know about his past. Tanner's next words disproved that.

"I was really sorry to hear about the death of that boy in your youth group." His voice dropped. "It's so hard to know what goes on inside a kid's head. Thank God He knows."

"Yeah." Jesse gulped. *He knew, so why didn't He stop Scott?*

"So you're taking a break from your ministry." Obviously unaware of Jesse's revolving faith questions, Tanner tilted back on his boot heels, his voice thoughtful. "Sometimes it's good to reassess if you're where God wants you."

"I guess Gran told you—" He stopped because Tanner was shaking his head.

"When it comes to kids' work I keep my ear to the ground so I can pray for all of us who are working with these precious souls." He grinned. "A friend of mine told me about your program in Colorado. Said you did amazing work. When he heard you'd resigned, he emailed me, ordered me to offer you a job if you happened by the area to visit Emma."

"That's kind of him," Jesse murmured.

"He's a man I trust, but he's not the only one singing your praises. Your grandmother has lots of stories about you, too. One day I'd like to see all those rodeo trophies you've collected, cowboy." Tanner chuckled at his grimace. "Okay, I'll drop it. Don't want to make you blush."

"Thanks," Jesse said with relief.

"Come on. I'll show you around." As they walked, Tanner explained that the focus of Wranglers was to reach kids through acceptance. "The man who owned this ranch, Burt, led me to God here, and many after me. His dream was for Wranglers Ranch to become a sanctuary, a kind of camp for kids. When he passed away he left this spread to me to make his dream come true. I started working with street kids because I was one once and I knew the impact this place could have. God's kind of expanded my puny efforts. Now we host church groups, kids from social agencies, kids involved with the justice system, kids who just stop by to see what's going on and sick kids, to name a few."

"Wow." Jesse was awed by such an expansive ministry.

"We use equine-assisted learning programs," Tanner explained. "We try hard to reach every kid for God, but, like you, we do lose some. Not every kid who comes to Wranglers Ranch is ready or willing to turn his life around."

"All we can do is shed some light on the path," Jesse agreed. "They have to choose it."

"That's why my friend was so impressed with your work. He said you made sure your kids understood what making the choice to be a child of God entails." Tanner then pointed out the horses in the paddocks, the land that stretched to the Catalina Mountains and the hands whom he credited for keeping his ranch functioning. "Wranglers Ranch is all about spreading the love of God. We use every resource we have to do that."

That simple explanation of such a far-reaching ministry sent Jesse's admiration for this man soaring and upped his desire to be part of it, a small part, anyway. But how to do it without getting personally involved?

"My friend said you have your degree in counseling." Tanner lifted one eyebrow.

"I went to college before I attended seminary," Jesse said.

"Actually, you started college on the expedited track when you were fourteen," Tanner corrected, a smile flickering at the corner of his mouth. "And left several years later with your master's degree in counseling."

"Yeah, I was kind of a misfit." It seemed Tanner had collected a lot of information about him, but Jesse wasn't going to add to it. It had taken forever to shed the geek label he'd carried in those days. He sure didn't want it back now.

"I'm not asking because I want you to do any counseling, Jesse." Tanner's quiet voice belied his probing look. "That's not what we do here."

"Then…?" He was mystified as to what his job might be.

"No counseling, but I sure wouldn't mind having someone with your credentials on-site." Tanner tilted his head to one side. "You're what—twenty-seven?"

Jesse nodded.

"You have education and life experience. You've worked with kids a lot so you have an advantage in spotting the kid who's good at hiding his feelings but desperately needs an outlet. You're probably more able than any of us here to spot the kid who's walking a tightrope of despair. That's what I want at Wranglers Ranch," Tanner said thoughtfully. "We need someone who'll catch the kid we've missed or the one whose needs haven't been properly addressed."

"I didn't manage that so well in Colorado," Jesse admitted, the shame of it rushing up inside.

"You didn't see your youth group kids' struggles?" Tanner's eyes widened in disbelief.

"Yes, of course, but—"

"You didn't go out of your way to talk to each of them privately, take them for coffee, spend extra time praying for them?" Tanner's probing was relentless. "Come on, Jesse. Tell me you didn't do everything you could to help each one of them."

"Yes, I did." Guilt ate like acid inside him. "But in the end it didn't make any difference, because I failed to save Scott."

"How do you know you didn't make any difference?" Tanner touched his shoulder, his voice quiet. "But whether you did or didn't isn't the point. We're called to show God's love. He takes it from there."

"I guess." Yet no matter how many months had passed, Jesse still couldn't wrap his mind around why it had happened.

"If you're still interested, here's the job. Work as a ranch hand. Offer as much love and caring as you can to every kid that comes to Wranglers Ranch, while keeping your eyes peeled for problems. If you find something that needs changing, you tell me." Tanner studied him, waiting.

"I see." Could he do this and still remain detached? Jesse wondered.

"At Wranglers we don't counsel anyone," Tanner enunciated. "Our job is first and foremost to befriend every kid who comes here, to make them feel this is a safe place and that we're here to help. Together we try to reach every child who shows up."

So maybe he could still be a kind of youth pastor, just in a different way, without letting himself get too personally involved with any of the kids. Was that what God wanted?

"I'd like to be a part of Wranglers Ranch." Jesse held out his hand. "Thank you, Tanner."

"Today's Friday. Start on Monday?" Tanner smiled at his nod as he shook hands. "Noah says you're camping out."

"For now." Jesse chuckled. "I had the impression Noah wouldn't mind joining me. He got this look on his face—I gather he's never camped before."

"No. His father wouldn't have allowed that." Tanner's expression grew solemn. "Maddie sometimes helps Sophie with our new baby, Carter, and Noah visits our kids a lot, so I've gotten to know the McGregor family fairly well since they moved in next door. Noah struggles to deal with his father's death and his list of unbreakable rules."

"Maddie told you about it?" Jesse blinked in surprise when Tanner shook his head.

"I've never heard Maddie talk about her husband except to say he died." The rancher inclined his head. "I did attend Liam's church once, years ago."

"And?" Jesse could hardly control his curiosity about sweet Maddie's former husband.

"Liam McGregor was much older than her, a stern man whom I thought was overly focused on details instead of God's love. I wouldn't say Liam found joy in his faith, more like it was his duty." Concern lay etched in the fine lines around Tanner's eyes. "His legacy of rule-keeping isn't helping Noah."

"Noah seems almost..." Jesse hesitated "...emotionally backward?"

"He's been diagnosed as a very high functioning autistic. After Liam's death, Maddie moved him from public school into a private setting to challenge him and to help his social awkwardness." Tanner's gaze turned assessing. "Noah probably feels like you did when you were so far ahead of other kids your age."

"Then I feel sorry for him." Jesse winced at the cascade of memories. "Social ineptitude leaves you out of the group, on your own and desperate for a friend. Except you don't know how to make them, and if you do, it's hard to discern which one is a real friend. You can't reach out, or you're afraid to in case others make fun of you. It's a lonely place and depression can easily creep in."

"And autism makes it ten times harder. I knew you'd be an asset here." Tanner looked pleased by his evaluation. "Wranglers Ranch is hosting Noah's class in a beginners' riding group next week. Both Maddie and Noah's teacher hope that working with the horses will help all of the kids relax their barriers, form some social bonds and develop a team spirit."

"A few riding classes are going to do all that?" Jesse asked skeptically.

"You've worked with horses. Didn't you ever feel the animals were a kindred spirit?" Tanner asked.

"My own horse, yes." Jesse smiled in remembrance. "In fact Coal Tar seemed to sense exactly what I needed him to do before I asked, but I raised him, worked with him for years."

"Here at Wranglers Ranch our animals are mostly abused stock that we've rescued. Maybe that makes them extra sensitive, but I think you'll soon see that as the kids work with their horses week after week, a bond develops. A kind of mutual trust." Tanner's self-deprecating shrug said a lot. "We've seen it happen over and over. Time at Wranglers Ranch with our horses always brings a change in the kids. You'll see it, too, Jesse."

"I'm looking forward to it." And he was. Meantime maybe he could learn more about his new friend. "Maddie seems very attuned to Noah."

"Her son is her whole world," Tanner agreed quietly. "Everything she does is for him, which is great but..."

"But?"

"But I wish she'd take more time to replenish her own well. Sophie and I keep hoping she'll accept your grandmother's offer of a partnership in her quilting store," Tanner said quietly.

"I guess that would help Gran, but maybe Maddie can't afford it or isn't well versed enough in business," Jesse suggested.

"She is on both scores." Tanner smiled.

"Maddie told us she purchased her ranch with part of a sizable life insurance policy she received after Liam's death, so she can certainly afford to buy the business. But the best part is the way she feels about quilts. She loves anything to do with them. She seems to come alive when she's working with fabric, as if the texture and pattern allow her to express feelings she usually keeps tucked inside."

"So what's the problem?" Jesse felt he was missing something. "Why hasn't she bought Gran's business already? I think Gran would sell."

"I believe Maddie refuses to buy out Emma because she lacks confidence in herself. From what she's said, I think she believes she isn't capable, and that simply isn't true. She's a very capable woman. I saw that when she was buying and moving to the ranch."

"Really?" Jesse was intrigued.

"Maddie had organized everything ahead of time. She prepared the house so the movers knew exactly where every box went. By the end of moving day, she had everything unpacked and in place, which I find astonishing." He grimaced.

"Why?" What was this about? Jesse wondered.

"Because it was nothing like that when I

helped Sophie and the kids move here after we were married. We still haven't unpacked some of her bags and boxes." His pained look said it all. "Maddie is detail-oriented, has foresight and considers everything from many angles."

"So?" Jesse waited, curious to hear the rest.

"I think Maddie McGregor lacks confidence because she hasn't ever had anyone to champion her, urge her to reach out of her comfort zone and support her efforts. In fact, judging by what I've garnered, I think she's been put down and deprecated."

Tanner didn't say it, but Jesse had the distinct impression he was referring to Maddie's former husband. The gourmet cook, he remembered, recalling Maddie's downcast face when she'd said that.

His new boss changed the subject by moving on to discuss hours, wages, staff meetings and a myriad of other employment details that Jesse only half heard because his mind was busy trying to put together a puzzle called Maddie.

As if he'd conjured her, she drove up at the end of his interview, as he was walking to his truck—which, he noticed with disgust, had a flat tire. She climbed out of her car and hurried toward him, her green eyes dark and shadowed.

"Hi," he said, a bubble of joy building inside his chest. "How are you?"

"I'm fine, but I need to talk to you, Jesse." Maddie looked serious. "About Emma."

His heart squeezed so tight he could hardly breathe. "What's wrong?" he asked, forcing the words out through his blocked throat.

"She's in hospital in Las Cruces." Maddie paused.

"What happened?" Panic gripped him.

"She was in a car accident. Among other injuries, including a fractured wrist, her hip was damaged. She's undergoing hip replacement surgery as we speak." Maddie's fingers rested on his arm, as if to comfort him as she continued.

"And?" Jesse steeled himself to hear the rest.

"Her friend Eunice, her passenger, was not badly hurt. She's the one who called your parents. Apparently they're flying in to see Emma. They asked Eunice to notify me at the shop, hoping I'd heard from you, since they knew you intended to stop in Tucson to visit her."

"Is Gran going to be all right?" The very thought of not having Emma there when he needed her sent a wave of devastation through Jesse. He gulped hard, lifted his head and found compassion in Maddie's gaze. "I can't lose her," he whispered brokenly.

"You're not going to lose her, Jesse." Maddie touched his cheek, forcing him to keep looking at her. "This is Emma, remember? She's very strong. You know she has a to-do list as long as my arm?" When he nodded, Maddie smiled. "Then you also know she's not going anywhere until that list is finished. Right?"

"Yes." He exhaled and smiled at her. "Thank you, Maddie."

"I'm praying for Emma." Her worried look returned. "But I'm very concerned about Quilt Essentials. Should I close the doors?"

"But…you've been running it for her. Can't you keep doing that?" Jesse asked.

"I've only ever taken over for a couple of days. Hip replacements have a long recovery time." Maddie looked scared at the prospect of handling the business on her own.

He didn't know why, maybe it was from talking to Tanner, but somehow Jesse had the utmost confidence in Maddie. "You can do it."

"How do you know that?" Her eyes widened in surprise.

"Gran trusted you enough to leave you in charge while she went away, and I don't think it was the first time," he added, feeling more certain by the moment.

"I've often managed the store if she had to be away for a few days, but—"

"Then just keep doing what you've always done." He smiled at her. "She'll come back to

find you've made her business better than ever."
He searched for a way to chase the doubt from
those turbulent green eyes. "My grandmother
believes in you, Maddie. So do I."

"You barely know me. But thank you for saying that." Her eyes glowed for a moment, then
darkened again, her apprehension returning.
"Except I don't think running Quilt Essentials
will be that simple and I don't think I can do
it for very long, though I guess I could handle
it for a few more days. At least until things get
sorted out. But we can talk about that later."
She looked as if she was mentally gathering her
strength. "You need to get to the airport now."

"I'll drive there." He made a face. "After I
fix my flat tire."

"A flat can wait. It's more important that you
ensure Emma's fine, get anything she needs,
and speak to your parents." Maddie's hesitation hinted there was something she hadn't yet
explained.

"Okay." Jesse tensed as he waited for whatever came next.

"If you leave right away you can return tonight and move into Emma's house. Somebody
has to stay there and take care of her babies."
Maddie looked as if there was nothing the least
bit unusual in that comment.

"Babies?" Jesse felt as if he'd missed an important kernel of information. "What babies?"

"The rescued animals." Maddie's green eyes widened again. "You don't know?"

"Uh-uh." Though he was impatient to get to Gran, Jesse knew he needed to hear this.

"Ever since her dog Buddy died, Emma's cared for rescued animals, ones that need more attention than the animal shelter can provide." Maddie shook her head to stop his protest. "Not medical care. She cares for the ones who need coddling or watching."

"Who looked after them while she was away?" Jesse asked.

"She hired someone to come in," Maddie explained. "Emma was returning home today because the caregiver flies out tonight to be with her pregnant daughter. Since Emma won't be coming home for a while, somebody has to take her place to care for the puppies."

"How many?" Jesse asked curiously.

"Nine. Newborns. Their mother died and they were left alone for at least a day before they were rescued. Emma took them in because they need feeding every few hours and lots of cuddling. The shelter couldn't manage that twenty-four hours a day." Maddie paused, then chided, "Are you following me, Jesse?"

"Yes. But I want to spend the weekend at

the hospital with Gran." Talk about a change in plans. More than ever he wondered what God was doing. "Isn't there someone else?"

"I asked, but the shelter doesn't have anyone. They're really short of help right now. Emma was their last hope to save those puppies." Maddie frowned. "They're not very healthy. They need regular feedings."

"I must get to Gran." Jesse was desperate to reassure himself that his grandmother would still be around to cheer and advise. He needed her sage advice and her tough love to help him find his way back to the faith that seemed so wobbly.

"I'll drive you to the airport," Maddie said. "But can you return tonight to care for the puppies? I can handle their six o'clock feeding, but not the night ones."

Of course she couldn't. Maddie was already going above and beyond by keeping Emma's store going. Jesse couldn't ask her to relocate to Gran's home with Noah, let alone get up at night with needy dogs.

"I'll deal with the puppies, but first I must see Gran." *Why Gran, God?*

"I suggest you leave your truck here. I'll drive you to the airport. I've reserved you a ticket." She smiled at his surprise. "Emma has a friend in the travel business."

"Thank you." He glanced at his truck. "I could drive myself—"

"Parking is really bad because of all the renovations they're doing," she said with a shake of her head. "It's better if I drop you off. You have to make this flight because it's the last flight of the day to Las Cruces. If you miss it you'll have to wait until tomorrow to see Emma."

"Okay." With no other option, Jesse made sure he had his wallet in his pocket, grabbed a jacket from the truck and climbed into her vehicle.

Moments later Maddie was weaving her way through traffic that seemed unusually heavy until Jesse spotted a road sign proclaiming this the first day of the Tucson gem show. That explained the excess of vehicles.

"You don't have to talk to me. Go ahead and pray for Emma." Maddie tossed him a sideways smile, then concentrated on merging onto Valencia Road toward the airport. "You're a pastor. I know you want to pray."

Yes, he did *want* to. But what had once come so easily was no longer so simple. What if, once again, God didn't answer as he hoped? Unable to even consider losing Gran, Jesse glanced out the window as he recalled familiar landmarks.

"How did your talk with Tanner go?" Maddie asked after some time had passed.

"As of Monday I'm newly employed at Wranglers Ranch."

"Good for you. I'm sure you'll enjoy it." Her smile eased the awkwardness of his inability to pray. "Tanner and Sophie are great."

"Sophie sure is an amazing cook." He patted his stomach. "She served chicken pot pie and blackberry cobbler for lunch. Delicious."

"I'm jealous. I had a peanut butter sandwich." Maddie laughed at his grimace. "Did you meet Wyatt and Ellie?"

"That would be Wranglers' veterinarian and his wife, the camp nurse," he said after a moment's thought. "I did. And the foreman, Lefty, and a bunch of others. Everyone seems very pleasant."

Another stretch of silence. Jesse couldn't think how to fill it.

"Oh, I almost forgot. I thought you might like a coffee, so I stopped for two on my way to Wranglers Ranch. That one's yours." Maddie indicated a cardboard cup in the holder with white writing on the lid. "Double cream, right? Like you had in your tea last night?"

"Thank you. It's exactly what I need." He sipped his coffee. Noting the excellent flavor, he checked the label, then let out a low whistle. "You must like coffee a lot. This place is the crème de la crème for serious coffeephiles."

Did her green eyes brighten? Her cheeks certainly turned a deeper shade of pink.

"Yes, well, I have a bit of an addiction to coffee," she confessed, her face averted.

It wasn't just because Maddie was lovely and gentle and sweet that he enjoyed getting to know her. It was all that and something more, something Jesse couldn't explain. He wasn't looking for a romantic relationship or any kind of involvement. But he *was* looking forward to broadening their friendship.

"I don't think addictions can be quantified as *a bit*," he teased, and laughed at her wince. "Fess up, lady. You've got a big obsession for coffee."

"I love coffee. Especially latte macchiatos. There. I said it. Are you happy?" Maddie being feisty was even more intriguing.

"Will you laugh if I tell you something?" Jesse asked sotto voce.

Her eyes widened when he leaned toward her. Her whole face was animated and her dark hair shimmered in the sunlight.

"I won't laugh, I promise. What is it?"

"After last night I was afraid you were a tea granny. You see, I only do tea with Gran or when there's no coffee." He couldn't suppress his burst of amusement at the relief flooding her face. He inhaled the aroma from his cup. "This makes the drive perfect."

But it wasn't just the coffee. Away from Noah, Maddie relaxed, laughed and smiled more. She'd removed the lid from her cup and Jesse smothered his grin when a sip left a puffy little cream mustache above her lips.

"You do realize that what you're drinking is not real coffee." Jesse enjoyed the way her green eyes expressed her mood. Right now they darkened with warning. "Latte macchiato means stained milk, so you're drinking mostly warm milk with a little espresso."

"It's *mostly* delicious and way better than that plain old regular double you're drinking." She defended herself with a mischievous grin.

"I'm looking forward to teaching you the delights of real coffee, Maddie McGregor." To that and a lot of other interactions.

She glanced at him, then concentrated on negotiating the car through the twists and turns of construction before finally pulling up in front of the departure doors.

"Thanks a lot for the ride," he said, before swallowing the last of his coffee.

"Please give Emma my love and tell her not to worry. I'll do my very best at the store. She must concentrate on recovering." Maddie handed him a small flowered box he guessed was candy.

"Please give her that and my love." Her amazing smile hit him like a jolt of electricity.

"Will do," he promised.

"When I pick you up tonight I want to hear all about her," she added. "Your return flight lands here at nine." The last sounded like a question.

"I'll be back," he promised. "But Maddie, you don't have to—"

A horn sounded loud and long behind them.

"I'll be here, Jesse," she promised, then shifted the car into gear, waiting for him to exit. "Your ticket's at the counter."

"Thank you, Maddie," he said, as he climbed out. "For everything."

She waved before driving away.

As they took off Jesse peered through the airplane window, watching the pink adobe houses that dotted the desert valley beneath dip away. He would enjoy coming back.

Because of Maddie?

You're not getting involved. Remember?

Maddie sat outside the airport terminal waiting for Jesse, wondering if it was too forward to have insisted on picking him up.

"That sign says we can only stay here five minutes," Noah warned. "Then we'll be breaking the rules."

"I don't think we'll have to wait—" She broke

off, struggling to stem her excitement as Jesse emerged. "There he is."

Why excitement? He was just a friend.

"Didn't mean to keep you waiting." Jesse climbed inside her car and tossed a smile over one shoulder. "Hey, Ark Man."

"Hi, PBX." Noah lost his stressed look.

Jesse chortled as Maddie pulled into traffic. Then she asked, "How's Emma?"

"Spitting mad." He chuckled. "She just bought that car—eleven years ago," he added in a droll tone.

"I can almost hear her." Maddie giggled. "She always talks about Beastie the car as if it's brand-new. Not that it's nice to have your car demolished in an accident, but—"

"Oh, it's not just the car." Jesse grinned. "She's also mad that her passenger got hurt, even if it was only bumps and bruises."

"What happened, anyway?" Maddie sobered at the thought of Emma hurt.

"Drunk driver." Jesse squeezed his eyes closed for a moment. "She was very fortunate."

"I know Emma," Maddie said gently. "And I'm quite sure she didn't give good fortune the credit for her survival."

"No. She's certain God saved her life because He has things for her to do. She'll be back before we know it." The way Jesse looked at her now made Maddie squirm. "When Gran returns she's going to press you hard to buy Quilt Essentials. This accident made her realize she has a long list of things to accomplish. She feels she must sell the store to have time to do them."

"Oh, but I can't buy…" Panicked, Maddie kept her eyes forward and swallowed hard. "I'm not a businessperson, Jesse. I'm trying to help her out, but I don't know anything about actually running a business."

"Gran says you know more than she does about quilts," he responded.

"That's only because I had a grandmother who taught me every quilting thing she knew." Maddie felt a rush of warmth at the memories. "My mother died when I was eight. When he had a job my dad would leave me with my grandmother. We had the grandest times. I guess that's why I love quilting, because it takes me back to that joy."

"She's gone now?" Jesse asked quietly.

"Yes." The depth of that loss still got to Maddie sometimes.

"And your father?"

"He died, too." She couldn't help the harsh way it came out. "Right after I got married."

"So you had only your husband to lean on."

How to answer that?

"I have Noah now." Maddie glanced in her son's direction. "He and I lean on each other."

"That's good." Jesse chatted with Noah for the rest of the drive to Emma's tidy adobe house.

"I need to get Noah home, but first I'll show you what to do for the puppies." Maddie switched off her car and pushed open her door. "I warn you, they'll probably wake up to eat at least a couple of times tonight. It's a good thing you don't have to start at Wranglers Ranch for a few days."

She inhaled the scent of Emma's blooming rose garden as they walked toward the house, but quickly turned back when Noah called out. She was surprised to see his whitened face.

"Are you sick, honey?" she asked in concern, remembering he'd acted oddly the last time she'd brought him over to check on the dogs.

"Do I have to go in?" he asked.

"I don't want you sitting out here alone." Maddie opened his car door. "You can help us with the puppies."

Noah made a face then left the car to trail reluctantly behind them to the house. With a sigh of resignation, Maddie unlocked the door.

"What's wrong?" Jesse asked in a hushed tone when her son quickly veered toward the living room.

"Noah's never comfortable with anything that

disrupts his usual patterns," she murmured as she switched on the lights. "I think the puppies scare him."

"Oh." Jesse studied Noah for a moment before asking, "Where are they?"

"In the laundry room." She raised her voice. "Come and help, Noah."

Glowering, the boy slowly walked toward her.

"I'm sure Jesse wants to rest, but if I show him what to do then he can get a few hours of sleep before the next feeding. If you help us, we'll finish quicker. Okay?" She waited for his reluctant nod. "Go with Jesse into the laundry room."

Noah still hung back, so after a moment Maddie drew him forward, trying to ease his nervousness as the tiny animals mewled around Jesse's feet.

"First we must change the papers." With Jesse's help she rolled up the floor covers and placed them in a bag, which Noah carried outside to the garbage. When he returned he had to be coaxed to help lay new ones, and would do so only after he'd folded them into triangles. Frustrated and weary, Maddie simply said, "Now we need to get their food ready."

She had done this only once, with the caregiver, but she pretended confidence as she demonstrated to Jesse how to prepare the formula the animal shelter had provided.

"Now for the fun part. Feeding." She smiled at her son. "Who's first?"

"Me." Jesse sat, leaned his back against the wall and cradled the tiniest furry body. "Hungry, are you, little one?" he cooed tenderly as he coaxed the puppy to latch on to the bottle. "That's right. Eat. But not too fast." He chuckled as the animal ignored his advice and greedily sucked the fluid.

"Your turn, son." Maddie touched Noah's shoulder, found it rigid. She didn't want to embarrass him, but—

"You gotta help me with these guys, Noah. After all, you're the Ark Man, in charge of animals." With his toe, Jesse nudged a pup closer to him. "Aren't they cute?"

Maddie had had little success involving Noah when they'd been here previously, but she persisted now because she so wanted him to have this experience.

"Come on, son. We'll do it together."

Attempts to engage Noah were not a success. He pulled away every time she tried to hand him a hungry pup. It was only when Jesse cupped his hands around Noah's and kept them there as Maddie set the next puny animal in them that her son finally cradled a puppy. His body stiffened at the touch of the claws, and he seemed frozen until Jesse began to speak in a calming, intimate tone.

"Good work, Ark Man," he murmured. "They're too little to hurt you, but they're hungry, so they claw to try to get the food faster. You have to hold their little feet so they can't scratch you."

Under Jesse's encouraging tutelage and effusive praise, Noah slowly relaxed and finally got the puppy drinking. Afraid she'd give away her delight at this big step in Noah's personal growth, Maddie left them to it while she retrieved the groceries she'd bought before she drove to the airport. She thought Jesse might want to have a warm drink before what she was certain would be a long night, so she set the kettle to boil and left a can of the hot cocoa mix that Emma preferred on the counter.

When Noah finally emerged from the laundry room, Maddie couldn't believe the transformation in her child. He looked—well, maybe not happy, but as if he'd overcome a barrier.

"They've all eaten, Mom," Noah told her. "I fed two."

"Well done." Maddie mouthed a thank-you to Jesse, who stood behind him.

"It's not bad once you get used to their claws," Noah mused.

"When we were here before you didn't even like them near you. What's different?" she asked curiously.

"Jesse said they'd die if we didn't help. He said God put people in charge of animals, so it's our job to help them." Noah's face scrunched up as he thought about it. "Jesse said the puppies make that noise 'cause their stomachs hurt 'cause they're hungry. I didn't want them to feel like my stomach does when it needs dinner."

"What kind of feeling is that?" Maddie asked. She'd never heard him speak so long.

To her surprise, Noah looked directly into her eyes. "Hurting."

"I see." A bit misty-eyed at this revelation from her often uncommunicative son, Maddie touched his shoulder. "I'm very proud of you for caring about the puppies, Noah."

"I'm the Ark Man, in charge of animals." His chest puffed out. He glanced at Jesse. "We're the caregivers."

"Yes, we are." Jesse held up his hand to high-five Noah, and after a moment the boy slowly returned the greeting. "We made up the middle-of-the-night feedings, too. Your very smart child figured I wouldn't have to stay up for so long if they were ready."

"Good thinking," she praised, privately noting that the former minister looked more tired than her young son. "I boiled the kettle if you want some cocoa. And there's a snack if you're hungry. I'm sure you know where everything is better than I do, so we'll get going home."

"That's nice of you." Jesse handed Noah a cookie, then bit into one himself. "Thank you."

"You'll set an alarm?" At his questioning look, she added, "So you won't sleep past the feeding time."

"I won't. I promise."

"Caregivers don't forget, right, Jes—I mean PBX?" Noah almost grinned.

"Never, Ark Man." He and Noah shared a look that brought a lump to Maddie's throat.

I don't know how Jesse's accomplished this, but please, don't let him leave just when Noah's finally beginning to come out of his shell.

Seeing the pair studying her with odd looks, she blushed, faked a cough, then said, "So we'll be off. Have a good rest, Jesse. I'll come and check on you and the puppies on my way to work tomorrow morning. Okay?"

Jesse nodded, but he didn't answer.

"Good night, then." She picked up her bag and shepherded Noah toward the door.

"Maddie?"

"Yes?" She stopped to face Jesse.

"Thank you. For everything. From me and from Gran, for the flowers you ordered for her, the encouraging note and for looking after her business. We appreciate it." Jesse's gentle blue eyes rested on her with an odd look that brought butterflies to Maddie's stomach.

He's just being friendly.

"Emma is our friend. So are you. Noah and I want to help both of you however we can." She said good-night once more then ushered Noah out the door and into the car.

As she drove away she noted that Jesse remained in the doorway, backlit by the lamps she'd switched on earlier to make the house feel homey.

"Mom?"

"Yes, Noah?" Maddie knew what was coming.

"I really like Jesse."

"Me, too, son. He's a good friend."

"Do you think Dad would be mad that I like him?" Worry seeped through Noah's quiet voice.

"What do you think?" Maddie temporized, having no ready answer.

Silence stretched for a long while.

"I think that if Dad knew Jesse, he would like him." Noah's voice gained confidence as he spoke. "Jesse talks about God all the time, about what He wants us to do and what Jesus would do. That's kind of like Dad, isn't it?"

Jesse was *nothing* like Liam. But Maddie didn't say that. Noah had taken an important step, made a new friend. Now, thanks to that dratted list of rules, he was having second thoughts.

"Is it wrong to be friends with Jesse, Mom?" His doubts made her rush to respond.

"No, son. Being friends with Jesse certainly isn't wrong." She hated feeling so defensive, then suddenly remembered a Bible verse from long ago. "The Bible says God directs our paths. I think God brought Jesse into our lives and He wouldn't do that if it was wrong, would He?"

"No. I remember Dad said God never does wrong things." Noah heaved a sigh. "That's good. Because I really like Jesse."

"Why?" Maddie asked, curious as to how Jesse had been able to reach Noah when many others had failed.

"He doesn't make me feel weird. Maybe I am kinda weird," Noah admitted thoughtfully. "But when I'm with Jesse I feel like he's okay with me being weird and then that helps me be okay with it, too."

Acceptance. That's exactly what Jesse had offered her, as well, Maddie mused as she drove onto her land. It was the one thing her father and Liam had never offered, the one thing she so desperately craved. To be accepted for who she was, faults and all.

To feel worthy of being loved.

When Noah was in bed, Maddie sat on her deck, staring into the desert as she organized her schedule in her mind. She was the longest-serving employee at Quilt Essentials. Emma had left her in charge, so keeping the store running was up to her. There were many things to think about.

Immediately, her body tightened with tension and fear took hold. What if she messed up? What if she did something so wrong that it cost Emma a lot of money to fix? What if Jesse was sorry he'd said he trusted her?

You need a protector, Madelyn. You're not smart enough to be trusted with anything important.

While she stared into the night sky, Liam's denigrations played over and over, until fear held her firmly in its grip.

"I can't do it, God. Liam was right. I *don't* know how to run a business," she confessed, pouring out her deepest heart, as Emma always urged. "I'm not good at being responsible."

She'll come back to find you've made her business better than ever. Gran trusted you enough to leave you in charge while she went away. My grandmother believes in you, Maddie. So do I.

Maddie stared at her solar butterfly for a long time. Then she took a deep breath and slowly exhaled, pushing out doubt and drawing in courage. Gaining confidence was her goal. Okay, this was the time to prove herself. With God's help, she *would* do this and finally repay sweet, generous Emma for all those times she'd listened and encouraged when Maddie had so desperately needed a friend.

Somehow it was reassuring to know that her new friend Jesse would also be there for her if she asked. But Maddie would do that only if she absolutely had to, because her days of being weak and needy were over. Hadn't she put away the romantic, girlish dreams she'd clung to all those years she'd been married to Liam?

She *was* learning to be independent and that meant remembering Jesse could only ever be a friend.

Maddie was never going to let anyone get close enough to hurt her again.

Chapter Four

Jesse groggily pushed his way out of a solar-butterfly-filled dream to answer the impatient summons of his grandmother's doorbell.

"Coming," he called, as he dragged himself up from the sofa where he'd spent the night. He needed a shower, a shave and a change of clothes, but because the doorbell kept up its persistent ringing he yanked open the front door, desperate for silence to quell the pounding in his head.

"Good morning." A vibrant Maddie stood on the doorstep, black hair gleaming in the brilliant sun. She wore a bright pink cardigan over a demure sundress splashed with tropical flowers.

"Morning." Next to Maddie's beauty Jesse felt like scum.

"I'm sorry to wake you. It's just that I need to be at work and I figured you'd need a ride to your truck and… Are you all right, Jesse?" Her glance revealed her concern.

"I'm fine. I had a restless night and fell asleep on the sofa." He translated her frown. "Don't worry. The puppies were fed, three times."

"Oh. Good." She stood there, gripping the handles of her green bag, obviously waiting for…?

"Sorry. I'm still a bit muzzy." He opened the door wide. "Come in."

"Thanks." Maddie's cheeky grin made him feel much better. "I'll put on some coffee if you'll change the puppies' papers."

"Mmm…" He licked his lips. "Did I mention I think you're an amazing woman? And that I love coffee?"

"I understand." She laughed, more of a carefree giggle really, but it suited her. "Strong double-creamed coffee coming right up."

"Thank you," he whispered, then paused as a new thought crossed his mind.

"Something wrong?" Maddie set her bag on the hall table.

"You, uh, said you didn't cook." Jesse didn't want to hurt her feelings, but he needed coffee to get him going in the morning and he sure didn't want to have to drink slough water. He kept his head averted. "So can you…?"

Hmm, not the most delicate approach.

"Can I make decent coffee?" Maddie said for him. He lifted his head and found her green eyes laughing at him. "Yes. I had to learn because Liam didn't drink coffee."

"And you're—ah, how shall I say it?" He widened his eyes.

"I can make coffee, Jesse. Very good coffee." Her narrowed gaze dared him to argue. Then she laughed. "Have to because I'm addicted to the stuff, remember?"

"I said you were amazing, right? And very talented?" He winked at her, closed the door and led the way to the kitchen.

Maddie opened a cupboard, selected a fresh container of coffee and opened it. Jesse paused for a moment to inhale the aroma of the fragrant grounds before he entered the laundry room to the whine of the puppies.

Thoughts of a hot, steamy cup of java kept him going as he restored the room to a semblance of cleanliness. He was about to snitch a cup of brew to sip before he mixed the formulas when Maddie appeared with a trayful of bottles and a very large steaming mug.

"I'm not the only coffee addict, am I?" she teased.

"Nope. Thank you." Jesse sipped the perfectly creamed coffee and allowed it to slide down his throat, hoping it would zip directly to his bloodstream. Then he set the cup aside, scooped up a puppy and began the now familiar ritual of feeding one hungry mouth after another.

"Even though you don't have triangles on the floor, I'll help you." Maddie giggled, then pulled a stool from the hallway and perched on it.

"But your dress—" he warned.

"Will be fine." She smiled at him, took a drink from her own steaming mug, then spread a large towel in her lap and lifted a puppy.

Jesse found something sweetly intimate about sitting here with Maddie in the early morning, tending to the puppies and sipping coffee together. It made him recall those daydreams he'd once had, silly imaginings of sharing his life with Eve. In fact, she was probably doing that right now. Only she was sharing with Rob, his best friend and the music minister in what Jesse had once called his home church. A lump lodged in his throat.

Lord, how could I have been so wrong about everything?

"Jesse?" Maddie's hand on his shoulder jerked him back to the present.

He pushed away the feelings of betrayal and teased, "Still here. Did you think I'd fallen asleep?"

"No. But the puppy has and there's another

waiting to take his place. Drink your coffee. It'll wake you up while I fetch you another dog."

She scooped the puppy out of his hand before he could object, and by the time he'd taken a small glug of coffee, she replaced it with another starving mouth and a fresh bottle.

With careful manipulation Jesse managed to wedge the pup and bottle in one arm so he could use his free hand to hold his cup, as he struggled to clear his brain of dreams that could never be.

Eve and I weren't perfect together because she never believed in me. Not really. Otherwise she'd never have blamed me for not helping Scott. How could she have thought I was working with him to feed my ego?

But she was right. I am to blame.

"So what do you have planned for today?" Maddie's gentle query brought reality's return as she selected another pup and began feeding it.

"Get my truck tire fixed." Jesse discovered that as long as he kept his eyes on Maddie, the day seemed full of potential. "It's very good coffee. Thank you."

"You're welcome." She smiled and that simple stretch of her pink lips lifted the heaviness from his heart. "I wish I didn't have to ask you to look after these fellows, but I didn't know who else…"

"It's fine. I'll catch some sleep later."

"What were you thinking about just now, Jesse?" she said in a very quiet voice. "Or should I ask whom?"

Normally he'd have brushed off the question or made some goofy response, but the compassion on Maddie's sweet face wouldn't permit a response that was less than honest. This must be why Emma loved Maddie, because of her caring concern, even for him, someone she barely knew.

"You don't have to tell me," she said in a self-conscious tone. "It's just that you've heard so much about my pitiful life that—"

"Your life isn't pitiful," he said sternly. "It's full of quilting and Wranglers Ranch and Gran's store and your child. By the way, where is the Ark Man this morning?"

"Noah's having breakfast at Wranglers. Sophie's making his favorite—waffles made in triangles, with blackberry syrup." Maddie arched her eyebrows. "You don't want to tell me your thoughts."

"It's kind of you to ask, but…" Though moved by her offer, Jesse didn't want to drag her down with his sad history.

"You don't think I'd understand." Maddie's whole face expressed her hurt before she ducked her head.

"No." He hated that he'd offended her. "It's me. I don't like to talk about my past."

"Me, neither." Her focus rested on something beyond the laundry room. "I'm trying to concentrate on the future, on my new life."

"As a widow, you mean?" He didn't quite understand why, but Maddie had suddenly tensed, as if whatever was in her past was painful.

"More as a new person, an independent person who is strong enough to build a good life for herself and her son." She frowned. "I'm trying to forget my past but—sometimes it seems like there are things you'll never be able to forget. Do you know what I mean?"

"Yes." He nodded. "In a way I suppose I'm trying to do the same."

"To forget the boy who died." Maddie said it gently, as if she thought the words would hurt him, but it wasn't the words that hurt Jesse. It was knowing he'd failed Scott. She handed him a puppy and a bottle and said, "You need a fresh group of kids to work with."

"No!" The word exploded out of him. Maddie blinked in surprise.

"Then why work at Wranglers Ranch?" While she waited for his response Maddie started feeding another dog.

"My parents raised four sons. My brothers are still there, ranching with Dad." Jesse didn't know why he was telling her this. He'd never shared a lot of personal details with anyone. "I was kind of an oddball kid. Never quite fit in. But then I had this…experience I guess you'd call it."

"Oh." Maddie blinked but said nothing more as she waited for him to explain.

"I'd been riding the hills and I stopped to rest the horse. I was lying on the grass, watching the clouds float past. Ever done that?" Would she understand? Jesse had never shared these memories with anyone, including his former fiancée. Because he'd somehow known that Eve wasn't the type of woman to lie on the grass and daydream about clouds.

And you think Maddie is? Because of that butterfly?

"I know exactly what you mean. I used to do that, too. Only I made up stories about the clouds." Maddie's eyes sparkled. "One was a prince swooping in to carry me away. Another was a house that was a real home. I'd always see a cloud that made me wish for a big happy family." She looked down, her lashes covering her expressive eyes. "Mostly I dreamed of freedom. Silly things like that."

Freedom? That tweaked Jesse's curiosity about the lovely Maddie, but he forced his brain back on the topic.

"Well anyway, I was lying there, watching the clouds, and all at once I just knew that God wanted me to work with kids." Jesse clamped his lips together. It sounded puerile put like that.

"How wonderful to know your purpose with such assurance." Maddie's voice echoed her wide-eyed admiration. "Amazing."

"It was, kind of." A rush of relief whooshed out of him. She understood.

"So you became a youth pastor? I know you'd be good at that because you have such a way with Noah."

"He's a great kid." Jesse felt a bubble of pleasure in having shared something so personal with Maddie. "Well, that's the last pup." He grinned as he offered her a hand up. "I promised Gran I'd take care of her babies, so when she emails you to ask, and she will, you can reassure her that they're being well cared for."

"You're doing a great job." Maddie's fingers clung to his for a moment as she rose unsteadily. "Thanks. My foot went to sleep."

"Better now?"

"Yes. I need to get to work." She tossed the towel into a nearby hamper before smoothing a hand over her dress. "If you're ready, I'll drive you to Wranglers Ranch now to get your truck."

"Maddie, you don't have to worry about me." A little spot inside him warmed at her thoughtfulness. "I'll call a cab. I don't want to make you late for work."

"I won't be if we leave soon. A taxi from here will cost you a fortune." Her forehead pleated in a frown as she checked the plain, cheap watch around her wrist, her concern about arriving late at Quilt Essentials evident.

"What if I tag along with you to Quilt Essentials?" A frown appeared on her pretty face, then melted into an expression he didn't understand. "No?"

"Of course that's fine. I'm sure you want to check that I'm doing everything right while your grandmother is away." Though Maddie said it evenly there was a hint of hurt underlying her comment.

"No, no. That isn't what I meant." Why hadn't he thought before he spoke? "I meant I could be there if you need me to do anything. Then, and feel free to say no if you want to, I thought maybe I could borrow your car to get to the ranch. I promise I'd have it back to you quickly. That way you wouldn't have to waste time driving me around."

She didn't look convinced.

"I really would like to help if I can, Maddie," Jesse insisted. "You've done a lot for me. I don't know anything about running Gran's store, and fortunately, I don't have to, because you're the one she entrusted that to. But if I can do anything to make it easier, I'd like to."

Maddie remained silent, her face unreadable.

"On second thought, my plan probably isn't that great. I'll rent a vehicle until I get my truck fixed."

"I think your idea is very generous and I'm happy to lend my car. But could we please leave soon?" Maddie checked her watch once more, frowned and shook her wrist. "This has stopped again." She walked into the kitchen and gasped at the time on the wall clock. "I have to leave!"

"Let's go." Jesse closed the laundry room, grabbed his keys and his wallet and led the way to the front door. "By the time I get back the dogs will be ready for another feeding. I'll do that, then go check out the truck. Will you need your car before two?"

"I have to pick up Noah at Wranglers at three thirty and take him to swimming lessons. He's having a special one on one lesson." She led the way to her car, got into the driver's seat and, when his belt was fastened, drove toward his grandmother's store. "We have a quilt shop hop running this week, so it's going to be a busy day. I hope no one calls in sick."

"A quilt shop hop? Is that a dance or something?" Her musical laughter made him think of butterflies and rainbows and possibilities.

"A shop hop is a kind of tour of quilt shops in the area," Maddie explained. "Guests bring in a passport that we stamp, and when they have it filled with stamps from different stores, they can enter it for a quilting cruise."

"A *quilting* cruise?" For a moment he thought she was joking, but her face said she was quite serious.

"I talked Emma into joining the other shops for that promotion. It's such good advertising. We've had a number of sign-ups for workshops when quilters stop by for the stamp and see what we have to offer." Maddie bit her lip. "Now I wish I'd kept silent. It makes for a lot of extra work."

"That's good, isn't it? You want more customers," Jesse reminded her. "That's another reason you should buy out Gran. She depended on word-of-mouth advertising, but you're up on current methods of merchandising that make it more fun for the clients. I noticed there's now a web page for Quilt Essentials. You set it up, didn't you, Maddie?"

"Yes. In high school I learned I have a knack for computer stuff. But—"

He chortled at her flushed face, amused by her embarrassment.

"You're a businesswoman." Jesse said it intentionally, hoping she'd realize what was so plain to him. "It's obvious why Gran thinks you'd make an excellent owner for her shop."

"Well, I love working there, but I can't own Quilt Essentials. It's too complicated and I'm not good at complicated."

Jesse thought of Noah's quilt and wanted to say, "Seriously?" But Maddie pulled into a parking spot beside the store and thrust the lever into Park. She turned to face him.

"I will do the very best I can to keep the store running while she's recovering. I promise you that. Now I must get to work."

Maddie gathered up her bag, a lunch container and a change of footwear, orange strappy sandals that showed a daring side to this modest mom, before exiting the car. He walked with her to the front door.

"I'll wait until you see if there's something you need help with," he said as she unlocked the door. "You're positive you want to let me borrow your car?"

"I'm positive." Her smile reassured him.

"Then thank you very much." Jesse watched her welcome two other employees, then explain about Emma's accident.

"I hope we can surprise her with what we accomplish by the time she comes back to Quilt Essentials," she said to the group, then introduced him.

Jesse shook their hands and tried to ignore their curious glances from Maddie to him.

"I'm sorry to rush, ladies, but we must restock the batiks before we get a rush of clients. Davina, can you get started shelving that new shipment?" She turned from the younger woman to the older one. "Anna, would you cut some more fat quarters from that new Kaffe Fassett fabric collection?" When Anna nodded, Maddie smiled, then added, "I'm going across to the warehouse to bring over some more kits. After Valentine's Day, if not before, I'll change the window to an Easter display. Easter's not that far away."

Valentine's? Easter? This was January!

Jesse almost laughed as the women moved to carry out Maddie's directions. He trailed behind her, out the door and across the parking lot to a space he knew Emma had purchased two years ago for storage. When Maddie noticed him following, she blinked.

"Oh, the car keys," she said with an embarrassed look. "I'm sorry. I forgot. We'll have to go back to the store."

"First let's get whatever you need here," he said, and held out his arms. "Load me up. I'm good at carrying."

"Thank you." With a distracted smile Maddie

selected a number of kits to fill a big cart sitting nearby. "We can sell more than that," she murmured thoughtfully. Jesse knew she wasn't talking to him as she selected another twenty premade quilt kits. "When our picnic basket project finishes next week, these will go like crazy." She dragged a second cart forward and filled it, too. "That's enough for now."

Jesse touched her arm, stopping her from manhandling the carts out the door.

"I'm here to help, remember?" He eased them forward, hooked one to the other, then paused to smile at her. "You know what, Maddie? Whoever told you you're not smart enough to run a business is just plain stupid. You're quick, you're intelligent and you know your market. All you lack is a little faith in the abilities God's given you."

"I—"

"You've got what it takes to make Gran's store better than it's ever been, and I'm going to keep telling you that until you believe it." He grunted as he shoved the carts ahead of him. "Now will you please show me how to steer this thing so I don't run down someone in the parking lot?"

Maddie studied him for a moment, then grinned. "You have to take off the brake," she explained with a chuckle. Something he couldn't describe flickered in her green eyes. "Thanks for the encouragement, Jesse."

"You're welcome." He made a production of getting the supplies into the store, but privately he thought he'd never had more fun. Maddie blushed at his outrageous teasing, peeked to see if the other two women noticed and told him to hush a couple of times. When everything was inside and the carts returned, he held out his palm. "Keys, please."

Maddie handed them over.

"You're absolutely sure you're okay with me driving your car?" he said seriously.

"I'm very okay with it," she told him. "Unless you're not back by three o'clock."

"I'll be here," he promised. "Have fun, ladies," he called.

Jesse drove away, surprised to note when he turned the corner to leave the lot that Maddie was still standing in the doorway where he'd left her, staring after him.

"Probably worried about me wrecking her car," he muttered.

But he knew that wasn't true. Maddie wasn't just beautiful. She was intelligent and kind and very generous. Who, he wanted to know, had tried to make her think she was less than that?

He needed to know so that he could be a good friend.

*   *   *

"You can't work if you're feeling ill, Jayne. I'll cover your shift." *How?* Maddie didn't say that into the phone. Instead she said, "I hope you feel better soon."

A moment later she hung up, focused on finding a way to deal with this newest problem. Staffing was by far her most difficult issue in managing Emma's shop.

Customers kept her busy for the next few hours, so that when she finally glanced at the clock on the wall she was stunned to notice it was ten to three. She would be able to pick up Noah by using the time as her lunch break, but there was no way she could be absent for the extra hour and a half needed for her son's swimming lesson.

I'm trying to help Emma, God. I'm trying to trust You. Can't You help me?

A customer interrupted her prayer and Maddie became engrossed in showing the woman how to rate the color values of various fabrics for her new quilt project. Only when that client left the shop did Maddie notice Jesse standing near the door, watching her.

"Hi." Why was she so glad to see him? She waited behind the counter as he approached her. "I didn't notice you come in."

"I'm not surprised. You were completely focused on helping your customer." He checked his watch. "When do you need to pick up Noah?"

"Now." She snatched her bag from under the counter, told her second in command that she was leaving and hurried toward the door which Jesse held open. "Thanks."

"Mind if I tag along?" he asked.

"Sure." Though Maddie was surprised by his request, she didn't have time to question it. He'd parked directly in front of the store so it took mere seconds to get in, buckle her seat belt and back out. "I can hardly wait to email Emma that the store is busy. We even had to find extra room for a class today and then it was bedlam."

"Bedlam? In a quilt store?" He looked unconvinced.

"Utter bedlam," Maddie assured him with a grin. "After a class, people always seem inspired and eager to shop for their next project. It's a good thing we have the new spring stock arriving every day because we need it. Some of the kids' lines—" Realizing she was babbling, she broke off to focus on her driving. "Sorry. I get carried away sometimes."

"It's nice to listen to you talk about your work," Jesse said. "You get this fervor in your voice that says you enjoy what you do."

"I do," she assured him. "Who wouldn't love

working in such a wonderfully creative atmosphere?"

"Then why don't you buy out Emma? Or at least go into a partnership with her?" Jesse's warm gaze studied her. "You're obviously a natural."

"Are we back on that again?" She shot him an arched look.

"Why not? It's a valid question," he retorted.

"It's true that I love fabrics and quilting. And I love sharing what I know." Maddie allowed herself to dream, just for a second, that she owned Quilt Essentials. Then she quickly shook her head. "But I wouldn't be a success at running the store."

Jesse frowned. "Why not? You managed today."

"A few days don't make me qualified to run a business."

"But you've run it on several occasions when Gran was away, right? You didn't have any problems, did you?" The intensity of his stare made her nervous.

"No, but I always knew she was coming back. Emma does the ordering. She has a personal relationship with our suppliers and she's developed a good rapport to get just the right blend of stock. I don't have connections like that." Maddie glanced at the clock and hoped Noah was busy with his video game and hadn't noticed she was running behind. She felt guilty, because she usually prayed he'd spend less time with the machine and more time interacting with people, and today it was her fault he wasn't.

"You build connections by being in business," Jesse countered.

"Besides that, Emma keeps a running mental tally of what we've sold each day. I'm not that clever with numbers."

"You mean…" Jesse thought for a minute. "Like, you haven't balanced the cash register these past few days?"

"Yes, of course I have." Maddie felt indignant at his implication. "We balance to the penny. Every day. It's mostly credit card receipts, anyway, so it's not hard."

"Then what do you mean, you're not good with numbers?" he asked.

"It takes a lot more than balancing a till to run a business." Maddie could tell he wasn't going to stop asking questions, so she began enumerating. "There's stock to purchase—not too much and hopefully not the wrong kind because we could get stuck with poor choices that don't sell and then we'd lose money." She glanced at him as she continued.

"Okay." His face encouraged her to continue.

"You also have to know the trends, keep in

touch with what's happening in the quilting world, innovations, et cetera. There are wages to pay, overhead, taxes, lawyers, accountants and staff schedules." She was out of breath. "Running a business is complicated."

"So you've thought it through pretty thoroughly." Jesse pinned her with a look. "Emma has a bookkeeper to help her. No reason you couldn't do the same. I think you're pretending to have a lot less skill than you do. Or that you've listened to someone who wanted you to think that."

Maddie frowned. What did he mean? Had Emma said something—but no, she knew her friend would guard whatever secrets she'd been told, although Maddie had never disclosed details of her troubled marriage. She'd been too ashamed.

"I think you'd make a very good business owner, Maddie. But I guess if you don't want to do it…" Jesse shrugged.

"It's not that. I'd love to buy Quilt Essentials and have my own business." Maddie couldn't stop the passionate words from blurting out. "It would be something of my own, something that *I* could make work, could build on."

A way to prove I'm not the airhead Liam always said I was.

But that negative thought drowned under

the plethora of ideas filling her mind. If she let them, the ideas would grow into fantastic dreams, but Maddie seldom allowed those dreams to progress. She stopped them now, as she always did, because she'd learned that there was no point in dreaming.

"So why don't you do it?" Jesse asked. "Where's your faith?"

"I'm afraid faith isn't something I have much of," she admitted, with a quick glance over her shoulder before she turned. "It's hard to trust God when it feels like He doesn't answer."

She expected Jesse to counter her comment with something ministerly, to tell her that God always answered, or some similar response. To her surprise he remained silent, his face thoughtful as he stared through the windshield. She wondered if he'd ever experienced the same unanswered doubts as she had.

Jesse Parker's faith is none of your business, an inner voice chided. Maddie swallowed a rush of shame that her thoughts were getting so personal about this man she barely knew. A glance at the clock made her catch her breath.

"You cannot be late," she muttered to herself, forced to brake because of the driver in front.

"A few minutes won't make that much difference," Jesse said. He took a second look at her, frowned and asked, "Will it?"

"Yes." She didn't intend to explain, but he kept looking at her so she finally said, "Noah's autism makes him very conscientious about scheduling. It upsets him when there are unplanned changes in his day. In his mind there's an order for everything and disrupting that order throws him off-kilter. He gets angry and uncomfortable."

"Ah. That explains his adherence to his father's rules." That thoughtful look again filled Jesse's face.

"Today's going to really throw him off because not only am I late picking him up, but I'll have to cancel his swimming lesson," she said with a frown as she turned toward Wranglers Ranch.

"Why?"

"One of Emma's staff phoned in sick. Two are on holiday and one is off on maternity leave. We're really shorthanded. I'll have to fill in the late afternoon shift."

"Added on to the day you've already worked?" Jesse frowned when she nodded. "I guess you can do that once in a while in a pinch, but it sounds to me like Quilt Essentials needs to hire more staff."

"We do. Emma was going to work on that when she returned. Now it will have to wait." Maddie couldn't get near Wranglers' main house where she thought Noah would be. She had to take another spot farther away. She could see Noah leaning against the fence, fidgeting, head down, shoulders hunched in the bustling midst of other more exuberant kids who were probably either beginning or ending a camp. He didn't even notice she'd arrived. "Oh dear."

She'd barely slid her fingers around the door handle to open it when Jesse touched her arm. "Maddie?"

"Yes?" She didn't want to stop and talk, but good manners prevented her from ignoring him.

"I could take Noah to his lesson, and back to Emma's house afterward," he offered. "I'd feed him supper so you wouldn't have to worry about getting back for that."

She wanted to say yes so badly. But Jesse was a stranger and Noah struggled with the unfamiliar.

"I don't think he'd go for it," she said, forcing a smile as she declined. "But thank you for offering. Excuse me. I need to get him."

Maddie hurried toward her son, her heart aching at his obvious confusion. She called his name when she got closer, but he didn't look up. When she arrived she didn't hug him as most parents would have. She wanted to, so desperately, but she knew Noah would shrink back. Physical contact wasn't something he needed as much as she did. In fact, touching made him antsier, so aside from a morning and evening hug, Maddie controlled her longing to hold him close.

"You weren't here." Noah's whisper barely penetrated the din around them.

"I know. I'm sorry I was late. Jayne called in sick at the last minute." Maddie shepherded him toward the car.

"Will she be okay?" Noah asked. When she nodded and opened the back car door, he stepped inside, pausing halfway when he saw Jesse. "Oh."

"I came along for the ride." Jesse flashed his Hollywood grin at Noah. "What's up, Doc?"

There was a pause. Noah frowned. "Huh?"

Maddie knew he didn't understand Jesse's colloquialism.

"Jesse means how's it going." She shot an apologetic look at her passenger, then when Noah didn't respond, clarified further. "He's asking how you are, honey."

"That isn't what he said." Noah buckled his seat belt as he thought about it, then responded. "I am well, thank you."

"Oh. Good." Jesse blinked at the very formal response.

"Noah, I'm sorry, but you're going to have to miss swimming today." Maddie drove between the ranch gates and into traffic, dreading upsetting him.

"I don't have an excuse to miss my lesson, so that would be rude." Noah's face tightened as he repeated another of his father's rules. "You never miss an appointment unless you're sick or in an accident."

"This is something like that. Jayne is sick and that means I have to cover her shift, so I can't take you to the pool today," she reiterated. "I'm so sorry, son."

"But I have my suit and towel and my goggles in my backpack. I'm ready." Noah began to fuss with his hands, agitated by the alteration in routine, as she'd known he would be. "I have to go."

"We can't today."

For the hundredth time Maddie asked God why her son had to have autism. It kept him from enjoying so much in life. Liam's rules only added to the burden of worry that deprived Noah even more, rules now so ingrained she wondered if her son could ever be free of them.

"Hey, Ark Man, I have an idea. Could I take you to your swimming lesson? That way your mom could fill in for Jayne." Jesse ignored the swift shake of her head and continued speaking. "I used to be a pretty good swimmer, you know. I even got my lifeguard badge."

Maddie so wished he hadn't said that. Noah often spoke of becoming a lifeguard, but that was so he could be in charge and make sure everyone followed the rules.

"I don't think—" She was about to brush off Jesse when Noah spoke.

"That's a good plan. He could take me, Mom. Then I wouldn't have to break my appointment." He sounded so serious.

"Well, Mom?" Jesse quirked an eyebrow. "What do you say? Tanner drove my truck to Emma's store, so Noah and I could go in it. You'd have your car, so you could take your time at work and join us at Emma's house when you're free. Noah could help me feed the puppies again, too. I would appreciate the assistance."

Maddie was about to refuse, until Jesse added that last bit. She recalled last night and the way he'd gotten Noah engaged in the puppies. She glanced at the youth pastor and quickly looked away. It was hard to concentrate on her driving with Jesse so attentive, as if he valued whatever she had to say. Recently she'd wondered if Noah needed some separation from her. Maybe it would be a good thing for him to spend time with a man like Jesse, who didn't stint on encouragement and praise.

"It's up to Noah. Is that what you want to

do, son?" She glanced at him in the rearview mirror, saw his forehead pleat as he thought it through.

"I would like to go swimming," Noah said. Then added, "And after I will help Jesse with the puppies, because I think he needs help. And so do the puppies."

Maddie wanted to squeal with delight. Noah had actually thought about someone else's needs outside of his own tightly contained world.

"Then I say thank you very much, Jesse." Maddie pulled into her parking spot at the store and switched off the car. "We appreciate it."

"No biggie." He climbed out and extended a hand to Noah, who hesitated a moment before grasping it and exiting the vehicle. "Friends help friends."

Maddie had certainly never had a friend like Jesse. What a relief that he wasn't looking for more than that, because she was never going to be vulnerable again.

"Have fun." She ruffled Noah's hair, then pulled a twenty-dollar bill out of her pocket and held it toward Jesse. "For pizza," she explained, confused when he frowned and pushed it away.

"You helped me. Now it's my turn to help you. Because we're friends. Okay?"

Maddie couldn't stop her heart from skipping a beat at his cheerful smile. In fact, she couldn't stop staring at him at all. All she could do was nod her head.

"You're a very nice friend to have, Jesse."

Chapter Five

Jesse hid a smile as Noah struggled to follow every one of his swim teacher's directions. The kid had grit. When the lesson was finished, Jesse added his praise to the teacher's, commending the boy on his determination.

"You're going to be a strong swimmer," he added as he drove to Emma's.

"I'm going to be a lifeguard." Noah stared straight ahead.

"How come?" Surprised by the resolve in his voice, Jesse waited for the answer.

"So I can make people obey the rules," Noah explained in a tight little voice.

"Why is that so important?" Jesse puzzled over his inner yen to help Maddie's son. He couldn't figure out whether that desire stemmed from his lifelong need to offer help when he could, or if it was because Noah was Maddie's son and she was his friend.

"Sinning is bad." It sounded as if Noah had heard those words many times before. "My dad said keeping the rules helps us not to sin."

"I guess keeping rules sometimes helps do that." Feeling as if he was about to tiptoe through a morass of theology, Jesse tried to explain his view. "I think not sinning has more to do with loving God and wanting to live the way He wants than it does with just keeping rules."

"My dad said you show you love God by keeping His rules." Noah frowned. "You think like my mom."

"I do? How does your mom think?" Jesse kept his eyes on his driving to hide his curiosity about that answer.

"She doesn't think rules are important." Again this sounded like something Noah was quoting.

"She doesn't?" Jesse gaped. "Are you telling me your mom doesn't think it's important if you make your bed or clean up your room or feed your dog?"

"Those aren't important rules." Disdain oozed from Noah's voice.

"They kind of are," Jesse countered as he drove into Emma's driveway. "Your dog would die if she didn't get food. If you don't make your bed you don't rest very well. And if you don't clean up your room, how can your laundry get done?"

He switched off the car, waiting for his passenger to digest that.

"I already do all those things." Noah unbuckled his seat belt. "Anyway, a messy room isn't a sin. Hurting someone is."

"Maybe a messy room hurts your mom." Jesse got out and held open Noah's door. "You don't want to do that."

The boy's jaw set in a stubborn line that Jesse struggled to understand. They walked toward the house, where Noah waited while Jesse unlocked the door. Something was going on.

"Because she already hurt a lot after your dad died, right?" Jesse hinted, unable to decipher the tension on the boy's face.

Noah shrugged, as if Maddie's suffering didn't matter. He set his backpack on the foyer bench, then motioned toward the laundry room. "Are we feeding the puppies now?"

"Judging by all the racket they're making, we'd better." Funny how Noah's impassive face lit up when he talked about those puppies. "You like feeding them now, don't you?"

"Uh-huh." Noah turned on the tap until hot water steamed out. Then he half-filled a pan with it.

"But you didn't before. Why now?" The kid behind that blank expression intrigued Jesse.

"'Cause they need me." Noah didn't even spare him a glance as he retrieved a tray of dog bottles from the fridge, opened the laundry room door and set them on the dryer.

Jesse set the pan of water beside the tray and placed the bottles in the water.

Without being asked Noah began to deftly replace the soiled papers with clean ones folded precisely in triangles. "I like triangles."

"I know." Jesse helped him, silently folding each paper in exactly the same way, waiting because he sensed that there was more this child needed to say.

"I'm important to the puppies."

Meaning Noah didn't feel important to anyone else?

But Maddie loved her son and she showed it. Puzzled, Jesse followed Noah as they took out the garbage. When they returned to the laundry room, he was surprised by the sound of the boy's soft chuckles.

"Look at them. They're greedy." When Jesse didn't immediately sit on one of the stools, Noah frowned. "Aren't you going to help me?"

"Of course." Breaking free of his thoughts, he picked up a dog, sat down and began feeding it the warmed milk. "Noah, what did you mean? You're important to Cocoa. She needs you."

"Cocoa doesn't need *me*, she just needs somebody to give her food and water." After that astute assessment, Noah began humming as his thumb rubbed rhythmically against the puppy's shiny coat.

"Cocoa is new to you and your ranch. It takes time to get to know each other. But your mom needs you. You must know that." Jesse took a chance and spoke his thoughts. "Both she and Cocoa would probably like it a lot if you hugged them, like you're hugging that puppy."

"Really? Why?" Noah lifted his head to stare, as though he'd never thought of such a thing.

"People and dogs like contact. Cocoa would like to be petted, have her tummy rubbed, given doggy treats. She wants you to pay attention to her, to need her. I'm sure your mom would like a hug, too. Everyone wants to feel like they matter to someone. Don't you?" Jesse wasn't sure where the words came from. He never was. He only knew something inside him compelled him to speak.

"I guess." Noah's glance slid to the puppy Jesse held. "Did you used to have a dog?"

"I've had several." Jesse let him remove the full pup. Oddly, Noah didn't hand him another animal to feed, but kept on feeding them himself. "One of them was named King, a black Labrador. He loved carrots."

"Carrots?" Noah's laughter echoed in the room. "I don't think Cocoa likes carrots."

"Maybe she hasn't tasted them yet." He watched Noah continue feeding, moving easily from one pup to the next until all the animals were fed. "You're very good with these guys."

"They don't understand what happened." Noah studied the animals now crowded together in a ball to nap. He slid his fingers over the satiny coats. "They're alone and they're scared." After a long silence, he added, "Sometimes I get like that."

"Me, too," Jesse admitted very softly.

"You get scared?" Noah's head jerked up. He frowned at Jesse's nod. "Why?"

"Everyone gets scared when they don't know what to expect. It doesn't matter if you're a kid, an adult or a puppy." Though Noah kept his gaze on the small animal cradled in his palms, Jesse knew he was listening. "When I get scared I pray."

"Why?" Noah's voice was almost inaudible.

"Because God doesn't want me to be afraid."

"Why?"

"You ask tough questions, Ark Man," he teased, then shrugged. "God doesn't want me to be afraid because it shows I don't trust Him to take care of me." Jesse could see by Noah's face that he needed to clarify. "It's like you and the puppies. At first they were probably afraid of you, but then they learned that they could trust you."

"But why does God want me to trust Him?"

"Because He's our father. He's going to take care of us, so He doesn't want us to fuss about everything." Jesse found a parallel. "Just like your mom wouldn't like it if you were always bugging her about having enough food to make supper."

Okay, given Maddie's less than stellar cooking skills, maybe that wasn't the perfect example. Noah's wrinkled nose said he was thinking the same thing.

"Your mother doesn't want you to fuss about having enough groceries because she already knows you need food to eat. She wants you to trust her to make sure you'll have it." Jesse rose, but kept his eye on the little boy.

"Dad always said Mom would forget her head." Noah put down the puppy and followed him from the room.

"I don't think that's true." Jesse couldn't let that negative comment pass without a challenge. "From what I've seen, your mother is very careful about remembering everything."

Noah didn't look convinced.

"She remembered my truck had a flat tire and loaned me her car so I could get it fixed," Jesse explained. "She remembered to make me promise I'd have her car back in time to take you for your swimming lesson, even though she's managing Emma's store."

"She doesn't usually forget swimming," Noah admitted.

"Because you're the most important thing to your mom. She would never forget anything to do with you." Jesse knew that was true. "She loves you too much for that."

Deep in thought, Noah left to wash his hands. By the time he returned to the kitchen Jesse was scouring his grandmother's stock of groceries.

"What are you looking for?" Noah followed every movement with his big knowing eyes.

"One last ingredient—ah." Jesse triumphantly located a can of pineapple in the back of Emma's pantry.

"What's that for?" Noah asked.

"Pizza. Want to help make it?" Jesse almost laughed out loud at the look of shock on the boy's thin face.

"We eat pizza at a restaurant. I don't think you can make pizza at home." There was a warning in Noah's serious response.

"Homemade pizza is the best, son." Jesse

grinned at him. "And my pizza is way better than any a restaurant makes. Want to help me?"

"I don't know how." There was that worry again.

"I'll show you." He winked, striving for some lightness.

"I'm not allowed to use the stove." Noah frowned. "That's a big rule."

"I'll do the oven part. You and I can make the pizza and when your mom comes to pick you up, we'll surprise her with our creation." Jesse wondered if the boy's father had ever taught him to consider his mother. "Having something hot and ready to eat will be nice for her after working so hard, don't you think?"

"I guess." Noah wore a confused look. "What do we do first?"

"The crust." Jesse grinned. "Gran keeps some of that made up in the freezer, so all we have to do is get the other stuff ready while we wait for it to thaw. How would you like to grate some cheese?"

"I don't know—"

"I'll show you," Jesse interrupted, grabbing a grater and then a hunk of mozzarella cheese. "Just like this, only watch your fingers. I don't like fingernails in my pizza," he joked.

Noah didn't crack a smile as, after a pause, he settled into the task. With serious concentration he carefully grasped the cheese and touched it lightly against the grater. When nothing happened he frowned and began to set it down.

"Push a little harder. You can't hurt it," Jesse encouraged.

Though clearly uncomfortable, Noah tried again and quickly got the hang of it. He created a huge pile of shredded cheese, far too much for one pizza, but the boy's satisfaction at completing the job was obvious.

"Good work," Jesse praised, when the last bit of cheese was gone.

"I liked doing that." Noah looked surprised, but Jesse didn't give him time to dwell on it.

"Now we need to chop up some meat for our pizza. Want to do that?"

"With a knife?" Noah's forehead pleated at his nod. "Knives are a major cause of household accidents. What if—"

"I'll show you how I do it." Jesse picked up a small knife and demonstrated how to cut a criss-cross pattern on the slices of ham. "We don't want big chunks," he added, then held out the knife. "Here."

"Okay." Noah exhaled heavily as if preparing to do battle. He accepted the knife tentatively, then with great precision began cutting the meat. "I like triangles," he said firmly.

"Triangles are perfect." The more Jesse

worked with this child, the more confused he became. Aside from gesticulating wildly when he was upset or frustrated, Noah did not usually exhibit the deep withdrawal he'd seen among the autistic children he'd studied during his college years. Noah was certainly high functioning and he didn't usually rage or have tantrums, so why had his father insisted on so many rules?

"Is that enough for the pizza?" At his nod, Noah set the knife down with relief. "I didn't get cut."

"No, because you were careful. Nice triangles." Jesse decided to voice a question that had been rolling through his brain. "Noah, do you have medication you need to take?"

Surprisingly, the boy made direct eye contact. "I'm not sick."

"No, of course you're not." Jesse backtracked, scrounging for a change of topic. "Is that your mom's car I hear?"

While Noah went to open the door for her, Jesse flattened the dough onto a pizza pan and tried to think it through. Maddie was a wonderful mother. She left nothing to chance. She'd said Noah was diagnosed at three. She would have had the diagnosis confirmed. She'd certainly know every detail in regard to her son's behavior. Hadn't his father?

"Hi, honey." The sound of her musical voice

sent a rush of excitement through Jesse. "How was swimming?"

"Good. We're making pizza." A flicker of pride filled Noah's words.

"Really? You're *making* pizza?" She appeared in the kitchen doorway and stared.

"Jesse is." Noah shoved his hands in his pockets. "I helped. I used a knife to cut triangles."

"Your favorite. Wow." Maddie sent Jesse a grateful look before she crouched in front of her son. "What else did you do?"

"Cut up cheese with no fingernails." In spite of his flat tone, Noah's eyes sparkled. "And we fed the puppies."

"You've certainly had a busy time." Maddie brushed her hand over his head as if she couldn't help herself. Her eyes glowed with love. "Thank you for helping. But we'd better leave now so Jesse can enjoy his pizza."

Noah frowned. "But—"

"You can't go," Jesse interrupted. "The pizza is for all of us. It's our dinner. Noah and I made it to share with you."

"But you've already done so much," she protested. "I don't want to impose—"

"You aren't. There's more than enough pizza." He held her gaze. "Besides, I think Noah should taste what he helped make."

"Would you like to stay for pizza?" Obviously

uncertain, Maddie looked at Noah, who didn't return her look. But the up and down jerk of his head was hard to misunderstand.

"Okay then," she said with a chuckle. "Thank you, Jesse. We'd love to stay for pizza."

While the pie baked Jesse squeezed some lemons for lemonade to go with it. Noah got involved on his laptop, so Jesse handed Maddie a cup of fresh coffee. He noted the way she arched her back to stretch it. And closed her eyes for a moment, as if searching for a second wind before facing the duties ahead.

"Busy day?" he asked.

"Very."

"That's good, isn't it?" He was confused.

"Oh yes. It's just that restocking isn't the easiest task." Maddie winced as she tilted her head to one side.

"Why is that?"

"Some of the shelves are too high and there aren't enough." She savored her coffee for a moment, then continued. "Emma's been talking of having someone build a better shelving system, but I guess that will be on hold for a while now."

"Not necessarily." Since Maddie was running his grandmother's business, Jesse figured he owed her any assistance he could offer. At least that's the excuse he gave himself. "I could build some shelves for you. I built those for Gran." He inclined his head toward the oak bookshelves he'd made several years ago to form the reading nook Emma had wanted.

"They're lovely, but I wouldn't want to interfere. Besides, it's your grandmother's business and she should be the one to decide..." Maddie's refusal died away when he shook his head at her.

"You got her email this morning, right? The one where Gran said to do whatever you needed to in order to make Quilt Essentials more functional? Besides, I'd like to help." He added ice cubes to the pitcher of lemonade and set it on the table. Then he grabbed a pad of paper and a pencil from Emma's kitchen desk. "Describe your shelves."

After a pause Maddie slowly began to explain her idea for a display unit. Her excitement grew and she talked faster and faster. Hiding his smile, Jesse sketched quickly, trying to turn her words into a picture.

"So this unit has four sides, all accessible?"

"Exactly." Her eyes sparkled. "I could really use it to display fabrics for the Easter quilt classes we'll be starting soon."

"What's an Easter quilt?" Jesse asked.

"A quilt that depicts the story of Easter in frames, kind of like stained glass windows. We've had a lot of interest in it ever since I hung the prototype." Her cheeks flushed and she tilted her head as if embarrassed. "I never thought anyone would want a class. I only wanted to make something to show potential for a new line of fabrics."

"Are you talking about the picture quilt I saw in the stockroom window, the one with the yellow trim? It had an empty tomb for the centerpiece?" Jesse gaped when she nodded. "You *made* that, pattern and all?"

"Well…yes." Maddie shifted uneasily under his stare. "It wasn't hard."

"It looks as if it has tons of pieces." The intricacy of that work had made Jesse assume it was a commercial quilt, sent from one of Gran's suppliers. "Are you sure you can teach someone to make that in—" he checked the calendar on the wall above the desk "—what? Eight classes? Easter's just over eight weeks away."

"You don't think I can do it." Her face fell and she resumed her familiar habit of knotting her fingers in her lap, her voice hesitant. "Maybe it is too big for a short class. I showed two of the other employees how to make it and they managed, but if you think—"

"What do I know about quilting? You have to teach it, Maddie," he said quickly, having just realized how he'd negated her ability. "Every quilter in town will sign up."

"I don't know. There are twelve panels," she

mused aloud. "They'd have to complete more than one a week to finish in time."

Jesse mentally kicked himself. Thanks to him Maddie was now doubting herself. He started backtracking.

"Aren't some panels easier than others?" he asked. "So if they did two panels a week they'd have lots of time."

"That's what I thought, but maybe that's pushing it. I don't want anyone disappointed. It would reflect badly on Emma's business." Maddie sniffed suddenly. "I'm no cook, but is something burning?"

Muttering an unflattering expletive about himself, Jesse raced to the stove and threw open the door, lifted out the pizza and switched off the oven.

"Is it burned?" Noah studied the pie critically, a certain resignation in his voice, as if he was used to eating scorched food, but had been hoping to escape that fate.

"Just one teensy part and I'll cut that off." His pride smarting, Jesse snatched the pizza cutter and swiftly rolled it to make eight big slices. "See, Noah. Triangles. Now let's see if it's any good," he invited.

"If not you might want to join my cooking lessons," Maddie teased, eyes sparkling again. "My first one is tomorrow evening."

"You're going to do it?" Jesse was surprised she'd have enough time. But then Maddie seemed to make time for the important things.

"I have to do something," she said with a mischievous grin. "Otherwise Noah's going to be a beanpole. He's always hungry and he's growing so fast."

When they'd gathered around the table, Jesse offered a quick thanks for the food, then served mother and son before selecting the burned section for himself. He caught Maddie watching him with an amused look and before he knew it she'd switched their plates.

"Hey!"

"The cook should always eat the best part." She winked at Noah. "It's a rule, right?"

He said nothing, his mouth full of pizza, his cheeks dotted with red tomato sauce.

"Bon appétit," Maddie said, before taking a dainty bite of her food.

Jesse waited with eager expectation, charmed by her altering expression as the flavors hit her tongue. She reminded him of a connoisseur, savoring the full nuance of the spices in the tomato sauce combined with the meat and pineapple.

"This must have taken forever to make," she said after she'd swallowed. "It's really amazing pizza."

"It took very little time, but that's because Gran had the dough for the crust in the freezer." Jesse served her another slice and grinned when she didn't refuse. "The topping is pretty easy. Anybody could do it."

"Maybe I'll learn how to make pizza at my cooking lessons." Maddie sipped her lemonade. "Thank you, Jesse. When I learn how to cook, I'll return the favor and make you a meal."

"I look forward to it." They ate the rest with sporadic conversation.

Jesse wanted to ask her about Noah's diagnosis, medication, everything. He'd hoped to find an explanation for the whole rules thing. But he barely knew Noah or Maddie. He might feel there was an unexplained reason behind Noah's reliance on those rules, but he could hardly pry into their business.

"You aren't camping anymore?" His pizza gone, Noah selected one of Emma's cookies, then re-formed the soft round shape into a triangle. When it was the way he wanted, he smiled before popping it into his mouth.

"No, but my stuff's still at the campground. I guess I'd better go get it." He shrugged. "I don't need to camp when I can stay here."

"But don't you want to camp anymore?" An intense longing shone in Noah's dark gaze.

"Camping's okay for a while," Jesse explained. "But it's nice to have a house you don't have to bend over to get into." The boy's keen interest gave him an idea. "Would you like to come with me to take down the tent?"

"Yes." Noah checked his response by looking at Maddie. "Can I? Please?"

"When?" she asked in a thoughtful voice.

"Next Saturday afternoon?" Jesse chose the date specifically because he knew she'd be working. "Noah and I can have a campfire, cook our lunch and then take everything down. After all," he cajoled, "I did promise him."

"Yes, you did." Maddie smiled at her son. "That's very nice of you, Jesse. Thank you."

"And mores," Noah reminded him. "You said we'd have mores."

"S'mores," Jesse corrected, repressing his urge to smile. He didn't want the boy to feel he was being mocked. "We'll have those for dessert. What's a campfire without s'mores?"

"Yeah." Though he obviously had no idea what they were, Noah's grin stretched from one cheek to the other.

"We'll help you feed the puppies and then we'd better get home. Church is tomorrow." Maddie rose and began collecting plates.

Sensing an opportunity, Jesse asked Noah to tend to the puppies, so he wouldn't overhear their conversation. When the boy was in the laundry room Jesse began probing.

"Maddie, I don't want to be nosy, but I wondered if Noah is on any type of medication for his autism?" he asked, as they loaded the dishwasher together. "I worked with autistic kids in college one summer and most of them had a prescription."

"A lot of autistic kids do." She turned her scarred face away from him, her voice soft but with an edge. "Noah doesn't."

"Oh. Okay. Good." He didn't want to press the issue because it felt like Maddie was withdrawing. Then suddenly, she turned and faced him.

"On his first day in kindergarten Noah acted up. He didn't understand why he couldn't keep coloring. Liam was embarrassed, said he was being disobedient, so he asked the doctor to prescribe something. After my husband died I told the doctors I wanted Noah off all medication that wasn't absolutely essential." Her voice was tight, as if she'd had to defend her decision and didn't want to be reminded of that. "It made him so groggy. He wasn't Noah anymore. Liam wanted obedience, compliance. I just wanted Noah to come back. When he was on the medication his eyes were so empty."

"And?" he asked and watched as she chewed her bottom lip for a moment while staring at him.

"It didn't seem to affect him," she added in a murmur. "He's doing well in his new school. Do you think I was wrong?"

"I'm not a doctor, Maddie, so I can't say. But I do believe God gives mothers great intuition about their kids." Jesse hated the pain etched in her lovely eyes, but he felt compelled to ask the questions whirling inside his head. "I guess you could always have him tested again. When was the last time you did that?"

"Before he started at his new school and then again before Christmas." Her voice dropped. "I track him pretty closely because I missed his first diagnosis." Her voice dropped. "I wasn't, um, well." Her head lifted, eyes glittering with tears of agony. "I had a miscarriage."

"I'm so sorry, Maddie." Why hadn't he kept his mouth shut? He was causing her even more pain.

"She was the prettiest little girl. Even though she was so small, I could see her beauty. I called her Lila." Maddie swiped away a tear. "Liam said it was God's will that she died, but I couldn't understand that. Why would God want my baby to die?" The last word came out on a sob. Unfortunately, Noah arrived just in time to hear it.

"Mom?" With a frown he stared at her, then at Jesse. "What's wrong?"

"Nothing, honey. I got a little dust in my eye, but it's gone now." Maddie forced a smile, hiding her sorrow as she no doubt had many times before. "Do you have homework?"

"Did it." He grinned. "Jesse helped me while we waited for the pizza dough to thaw out."

"Was it art class again?" There was a hesitant note in Maddie's voice that Jesse didn't understand. Noah did, though, and he wore an ear-splitting grin as he nodded.

"Farm animals," he said, clearly enjoying it when she groaned.

"It seems I owe you yet another thank-you, Jesse. Even double thanks."

"For helping draw animals?" He shrugged. "No problem."

"It is to me." Maddie's chagrin was obvious. "I can't draw anything but stickmen and even they look odd."

"But you do quilts good." Noah awkwardly hugged her side, bumping against her hip like an awkward calf before he moved away, head bent, so he didn't see the surprise and pleasure filling his mother's face at the unexpected contact.

But Jesse did.

"Thank you, son." Maddie's eyes welled, but she dabbed away the tears. "That's very kind of you to say. Now you'd better grab your back-pack so we can get home. And don't forget to thank Jesse."

Noah did thank him. Effusively. And reminded him of his promise for next Saturday.

"It's a date," Jesse agreed.

"Thank you so much," Maddie said with a big smile. "For everything. It's been like old times to have supper at Emma's." Her face clouded. "I'm just sorry she's not here to share it."

"According to my parents, with the progress she's making she will be soon. And then Noah and I will make her our special pizza." He ruffled the boy's hair, and though Noah ducked away, Jesse knew he didn't really mind.

"That sounds great." Maddie took Noah's hand. "Okay, we're off. Thanks again."

"See you Monday," he called.

She stopped, turned and stared at him with a frown.

"To build the shelves," he reminded her, then waved off her protests. "I'll be there first thing in the morning."

"Oh. Well, thank you. Again." She opened the door, but Noah slipped under her arm and raced back to Jesse.

"I think she liked the hug," he whispered, eyes downcast.

"I know she did. You could do it more often."

"Really?" Noah frowned, then shot him a quick grin before scurrying out the door.

Jesse watched them drive away. All in all, a very good evening, he decided. He'd found the answers he'd wanted. The boy's father had been a stickler for rules. But Jesse wasn't sure that would help him understand Noah any better. It had, however, whetted his appetite to know more about sweet Maddie. In fact, his questions about her were growing exponentially.

If he pressed her too hard for more information about Noah, she'd probably blame herself again. That was the last thing Jesse wanted to see happen.

Funny how Maddie's emotional state was becoming so important to him.

Chapter Six

"It's very kind of you to build the shelves." Maddie stood in the middle of the store, arms loaded with bolts of colorful fabric, looking remarkably unruffled amid what seemed to Jesse to be pure chaos. "Especially after working all day at Wranglers."

"No problem. I just wish I could have made it Monday instead of making you wait till Thursday." He glanced around. "Can I come and go using the back door? I'll leave the saws out there."

"Sounds fine." Her smile was distracted. "Today's our afternoon piecing class, so for the next few hours we'll mostly be in the workroom. Excuse me, I'd better get this fabric cut."

He nodded, fascinated to watch her work. Each client got Maddie's complete attention. She listened to what they said then offered advice and suggestions that made each encounter very personal. Every single customer left smiling.

Jesse broke free of his musings and left after Maddie shot him a curious look. As he paused to check on the puppies sleeping in their box in the shaded truck, the door opened and the echo of laughter and happy chatter burst toward him. He smiled at the sounds of fun that emanated from Quilt Essentials as he unloaded wood, rechecked his measurements and began constructing. Gran would love to be here, though her emails said without words that she had all she could handle with her recovery.

"Thank You God for Maddie," he whispered.

As Jesse sawed and hammered in the back parking lot, he enjoyed the lovely breeze that kept his shady spot from becoming too hot. He'd just finished assembling the base for the unit when Maddie appeared.

"Coffee time." She held out a big steaming mug, then frowned. "You're welcome to drink it inside if you want."

"Thanks, but it's such a gorgeous day that it's a pleasure to be outdoors." He accepted a napkin holding two cookies, then sat on the tailgate of his truck, surprised when she joined him. "Your class sounds like a lot of fun."

"They always are," she agreed with a smile.

"Though it gets a little hectic trying to make sure everyone's following directions, especially when it's first-timers trying our Bargello pattern."

"I'm not even going to ask you to explain that." Jesse grinned at her, enjoying the relaxed sense of camaraderie. "I should be ready to start putting pieces for the new unit in place soon, if that's okay."

"It's great. There's no class tonight." She studied his first-stage construction. "It looks exactly as I wanted. Have you always known how to build?"

"Dad started us young. When you live on a ranch that's miles from town you have to be able to repair and reuse what you have as well as make what you need." He shrugged. "I'm nowhere near as good a carpenter as he is but I try."

"And your brothers—are they good carpenters?" She looked startled when he made a face. "I'll take that as a no."

"Mac prefers the rodeo. Dan prefers breeding his Black Angus cattle and Rich…" Jesse wasn't exactly sure how to say this to her. "Rich prefers the ladies."

"Your face is red," she said with a chuckle.

"Rich is kind of embarrassing sometimes." He ducked his head and drank his coffee.

"After you left your church—you didn't want to stay and ranch with your family?" Maddie's long black lashes hid her eyes, but he could hear the questions in her voice.

"I wanted to leave Colorado as fast as I could." He tired to hide his frustration.

"Because?" She did look at him then.

"Because I knew I was to blame for that death. I knew I hadn't done enough to save Scott." He debated saying the next part, but something in him needed to verbalize his miasma of feelings. "But if I was to blame, so was God."

Maddie didn't gasp, stare at him or call him sacrilegious as his former fiancée had. Instead she seemed to be considering his words.

"Because He didn't stop it from happening, you mean?" she finally asked.

"Yes." Jesse felt great relief that she understood without more explanation, but he also hated that such thoughts had ever taken root in his head. Maybe Eve was right. Maybe being blamed was his punishment for questioning God.

"I felt the same way when Noah was diagnosed." Maddie's retrospective tone broke into his thoughts. "I did everything I could to have a healthy baby. And yet Noah had problems. Liam said it was a genetic problem on my side, that it had to be because there weren't any autistics in his family." Her voice dropped to a whisper. "For years I couldn't understand why God had done that to me, punished me like that."

"Do you understand now?" Jesse asked curiously.

"Understand why Noah has problems?" She turned her head sideways to study him. "No. But thanks to Sophie I am beginning to accept that it doesn't matter, just as it doesn't matter why her daughter, Beth, has Down syndrome. Noah is who he is. What matters is loving both of them for who they are and helping them become all that they can be."

"Meaning?" In Maddie Jesse saw a maturity he hadn't anticipated. Though Noah was only eight, his mother seemed focused on his personal growth. From his youth group work Jesse knew some parents never understood their focus had to be on their kid.

"Liam wanted Noah to be a copy of himself. Top of the class, a leader, strong, competent." Her voice was soft, hesitant.

"And you don't?" Jesse's heart squeezed at her gentle smile when she shook her head.

"I want Noah to be Noah. I want him to experience the joys of life, to feel others' pain so he won't cause it. I want him to grow up understanding that life isn't about being the smartest or the fastest or the richest." Her voice gathered strength as she spoke. "I am determined to help my son realize that when you give to others you are far richer than any money can make you. I want him to understand that a good friend will help and support you and that you can do the same for him. In other words, I want Noah to be the best he can be. Whatever that is."

"I think Noah got a wonderful mom when God chose you." Jesse's praise was genuine.

"Thanks." She blushed most charmingly. "It sounds grandiose and I'm not at all sure that I can do it. But that's my goal."

"But what about for you? What do you want for yourself?" he probed, thinking of Tanner's comments from the first day Jesse had gone to Wranglers Ranch.

"I don't need anything," she said, after a few moments had passed.

"That isn't what I meant. I was asking what Maddie McGregor dreams of for herself. What wonderful things do you want to be and do and say?" Jesse could tell by her nonplused mien that she'd long since put away her dreams. "You're young and strong. You're gifted with fabric. You're determined to learn what you don't know and you're great with people. So what do you see yourself doing in ten years, Maddie? Or when Noah grows up and is involved in his own busy life."

She stared at him for a long time. During those moments a hundred different reactions chased across her face: hope, optimism, possibilities. Then someone from inside the store called her name and the flare of excitement died as quickly as a fire doused with water.

"I'll just keep being plain old me, I guess." She scooted off the tailgate and picked up his empty cup.

Jesse couldn't let her go like that, couldn't let the first flicker of dreams he'd glimpsed in those green eyes die, so he waited until she had almost reached the corner of the building.

"I'd argue that word *plain*, Maddie," he said seriously. "But don't you want more? Don't you want to discover all the wonderful things God has planned for *you* to do with the rest of your life?"

She turned to look at him as if he'd suggested she make a quilt out of old shoes. Then she shrugged.

"I don't think God has planned much more for me than to be Noah's mom." Her voice was quiet, reflective. "Otherwise He'd have given me the qualifications to be something great. But that's okay, because being Noah's mom is a great enough job for me." She smiled at him before pointing out, "The puppies want feeding."

Then she turned and went inside the shop.

Moments later a burst of laughter echoed from the building.

Oh, Maddie. Jesse's heart dropped to his feet as he lifted the dogs one by one and fed them with the bottles tucked into the cooler he'd brought. *You have so much to give and you don't even know it.*

Maybe he could show her that her dreams were achievable.

Except you're not getting involved, his brain reminded him.

So he wouldn't get involved, Jesse reasoned. He'd just use every opportunity he found to point out to Maddie that she already had the abilities she needed to reach for her dreams in spite of what her negative husband had drummed into her.

While he was here he'd do what he could to help. But when Gran returned and was settled at home, Jesse would leave Tucson and Maddie and Noah. Maybe by then he'd have found the answer to his question—why had God let Scott die?

"You look comfy, but I think those puppies are wearing you out." On Saturday evening Maddie studied Jesse, who sat flopped in a canvas chair beside a flickering campfire.

"I can't get used to the interrupted nights."

He stifled his yawn. "But the dogs are growing. It won't last forever."

"I hope you last." She glanced to the side, where Noah was exploring Jesse's tent. "Thanks for putting off Noah until I could get here. I'm curious to see his reaction."

"Hard to tell, since he hasn't yet come out of the tent." For a moment Jesse wore a yearning look, as if he wanted to climb into that tent, crawl into his sleeping bag and dream. But then his blue eyes began to twinkle. He tossed his head back to shift his sandy hair out of his eyes. "You never said how your first cooking class went."

"I was afraid you'd ask." Maddie stopped her groan midway and made a face instead. "Horrible."

"What did you make?" Jesse looked so confident and strong, as if he never doubted himself.

"A boiled egg." She felt like a wimp. An incompetent wimp.

"How could a boiled egg..." She must have shown her distress because he stopped and shook his head. "Never mind."

"I dropped the first one on the floor." Maddie felt her cheeks burn with shame. "The second one I dropped into the pan. The white bubbled all over, so I only had a little ball of yolk left to put on my toast."

"Oh, dear." Jesse's shoulders hunched as he gave a sort of strangled cough.

"Stop laughing. It was awful." Maddie confessed the rest of her disastrous evening at the cooking school and her shame as the other students tried to help her. "Nobody else was as incompetent as me. But I'm going to do better," she said, thrusting up her chin.

"Of course you will. Cooking's just a matter of practice." Jesse could barely contain his amusement when Noah stuck his head between the tent flaps to say he wanted boiled eggs for breakfast.

"Not tomorrow, son. I need another lesson first."

"Prob'ly more than one." Noah's sigh said it all before he ducked back inside the tent. Jesse's chuckle drew heads from several other campsites.

"I'm laughing with you, not at you." His words did little to make her feel better. "You're a good sport, Maddie."

She gave him a dubious scowl.

"You're hungry. Let's cook some hot dogs." He called Noah to help him find sticks while Maddie unpacked the picnic basket he'd brought.

"We're ready," he said, when they returned with three sticks. With painstaking care, he explained to Noah how he'd sharpen the end so they could press on the meat. "Then you hold it very carefully over the fire. Don't let it get too near the flame or it will burn."

"Hey, maybe if we had hot dogs every night I wouldn't need cooking lessons," Maddie murmured. Noah looked ecstatic, but Jesse shook his head.

"You'd get bored with them after a while. Then they wouldn't be a treat anymore," he warned.

"I guess." With that way of escape blocked, Maddie focused on a new kind of cooking. She followed Jesse's instructions to the letter, but to her dismay lost the first two hot dogs to the fire. "I knew that would happen." Chagrined, she was ready to toss her stick and eat the wiener cold, but Jesse wouldn't let her.

"Maddie, you've got to stop thinking so negatively." He frowned at her. "Accidents happen to everybody."

"It didn't happen to you." She loved the calm, patient way he adjusted Noah's grip so he wouldn't suffer the same loss she had.

"I've done this before. Hundreds of times." Jesse handed her a loaded stick and made himself another. "But imagine if I were to make a quilt. There'd be lots of mistakes and you wouldn't think there was anything wrong with that because I've never made one before."

"Yes, but I can't—"

"Stop saying that. It's not that you can't cook," Jesse continued. "It's just that you've never learned. But you're smart. You *can* learn. You just have to be more positive."

"I do?" She stared at him, intrigued by the reassurance in his words.

"Of course. God doesn't create failures, Maddie. He knew all about us before we were even born and He knows what we need to learn. He doesn't call us dumb." Jesse lifted his head from his perusal of the fire. A lock of sandy hair flopped over one eye, giving him a rakish look she liked. "One of God's names is Jehovah Shammah, which means 'the Lord is there.' As in, 'I'm here to help you. Try again.'"

"I never thought of that." Feeling self-conscious, Maddie thought the setting sun made the campsite seem more intimate. "I've always felt like I've failed God."

"We all fail him." There was a smile in Jesse's voice. "Fortunately, God gives do-overs."

"Yeah."

A lightness filled her heart until a quiet voice said, "Burning."

Maddie lifted her head to see Noah's hot dog in flames. She couldn't help laughing at her son's offended look when the charred meat tumbled into the fire.

"I'm sorry, honey, but you and I are fiascos at this camping thing."

"'Cause we need practice." Noah shot her a wily grin. "Do-overs."

Surprised that he'd followed their conversation so closely, she glanced at Jesse, who, with eyes twinkling, handed her his own golden-roasted wiener in a thick fluffy bun.

"Go for it," he said. Then he rose to get Noah a replacement hot dog. He'd barely threaded that onto Noah's stick when the puppies started crying.

Knowing Jesse must be hungry after hours of labor at Emma's shop, Maddie handed him the hot dog. "Eat it," she insisted. "Then you can roast me another after I feed the puppies."

"That's not exactly learning the camping skill I was trying to teach," he chided, but when she wouldn't take it back he bit into it gratefully.

"I'll learn it another time. I promise I will not give up on this. Anyway, I doubt Noah would let me." She winked at him, ignoring the inner voice that chided her for such a brazen act, then began feeding a pup. It seemed only moments later that Noah reached out for the now satiated dog.

"Our turn." Jesse held out a steaming hot dog. "You eat. We'll finish feeding these guys then we'll make some s'mores." He nodded at Noah, who'd sunk onto a nearby log and was cooing gently at the puppy he was feeding. "Looks like he's become attached. You might have trouble giving them away."

"I hope not." She blinked. "I certainly can't keep nine puppies."

While Maddie savored the perfectly roasted hot dog, she studied Jesse and Noah. They teased each other about who was doing the best job feeding, and yet with every comment Jesse infused encouragement into his words. His calm certainty and compliments seemed to rejuvenate Noah, who didn't hang his head or avoid looking at Jesse. In fact, he became more engaged, especially when Jesse set the last dog back in the box and announced it was s'mores time.

She wanted to laugh as the two males soberly and with great ceremony arranged the supplies on the picnic table: graham wafers, huge fluffy marshmallows and four chocolate bars.

"Four?" she asked in surprise.

"I think we'll be having seconds, Mom." Noah gave her a bold grin. "Maybe thirds." Then he frowned. "Okay?" His hesitation nearly broke her heart.

"Okay with me," she choked out. "As long as you don't make yourself sick, and as long as you don't do it every night."

Noah nodded happily then focused on Jesse

who broke the bars into pieces before skewering a marshmallow on a stick.

"So we make s'mores by roasting the marshmallow golden brown, which isn't easy to do," he warned. "Because they catch fire if you're not careful."

"I'll be careful," Noah promised. "Then what?"

"Then we put the melted marshmallow on a cracker that has a piece of chocolate on it. We put another cracker on top and wait till the chocolate melts. And then we eat it. Watch," he invited, and demonstrated, patiently answering Noah's repeated question of—

"Is it ready yet?"

Finally, it was. Jesse put the treat together, then held it out to Noah. Surprisingly, the boy shook his head.

"You made it so you should eat it." Noah's dark eyes widened as Jesse took a bite, chewed thoroughly, then scooped the melting chocolate from the corner of his mouth with his tongue. "I wanna make my own. But I like triangles better than squares."

"We can make the cracker into a triangle but it'll be pretty small for these big marshmallows. Want to try?" Jesse experimented and ended up with a tiny morsel that made Maddie laugh. When she and Noah both lost their marshmallows to the fire he shrugged. "It happens. Try again."

They did try. Noah caught on right away and was soon savoring his treat, edges reshaped into a triangle. But Maddie's next two marshmallows turned to charred cinders and fell into the coals before she finally toasted one golden brown.

"Now that's edible." Jesse applauded.

The sickly sweet, sticky dessert wasn't her favorite, but she enjoyed every morsel because Jesse was there, making this a special occasion for Noah.

"One more?" Noah pleaded when Jesse began putting the s'more supplies away.

"Maddie?" Jesse waited for her nod of approval. "Go ahead, son. You have just enough time," he told Noah.

"Huh?" Noah thrust the marshmallow on the stick.

"After we have s'mores I usually have a sing-along around the campfire." Jesse studied the boy's blank look. "You don't know what a sing-along is?"

"Singing?" He shrugged in disinterest then moved to toast his marshmallow. He was savoring his final s'more when Jesse lifted a guitar from his truck.

Noah froze. Maddie watched his eyes stretch wide.

"You play guitar? Cool," he breathed.

"You like guitars?" Jesse strummed a few chords. "They're easy to learn to play." He demonstrated with the first line of a popular church chorus. "See? It's not hard. Want to try?"

Maddie held her breath. She'd never seen Noah so captivated. He wore a rapt look as Jesse told him to sit on the bench of the picnic table, placed the guitar in his lap and set his hands on the instrument. Noah was eight, and in all those years she'd never noticed his interest in a guitar or anything musical. How had Jesse known how to reach him?

Though she fought to keep her face impassive, her heart thudded with joy as Jesse showed Noah how to play his first chord. A sandy-colored head huddled next to a dark brown one as Noah listened to Jesse's instructions and then, encouraged by the former youth minister, strummed a few tentative strokes across the strings. He beamed with delight at the sound.

"I played something!" His eyes glowed with pleasure.

"Of course you did." Jesse ruffled his hair. "You're a smart kid."

Before long Noah was playing a simple song and humming along. Curious about his reaction, Maddie finally asked, "Do you like the guitar?"

"Yes." Noah paused, and his face tightened.

After several moments' thought he frowned then held out the guitar to Jesse. "Playing this is wrong. It's against the rules."

"It is?" Jesse carefully stored the guitar in the truck and returned. "God gave us music. How could it be wrong?"

Maddie wanted to hear the answer to that. Maybe it would shed light on what had troubled Noah since his father's death.

"It was such a lovely song," she said softly. "Why do you think it's wrong?"

"'Cause." All joy in the wonderful evening drained from his face, leaving his eyes dark and empty. "Dad said music should worship God in hymns. That wasn't a hymn." His voice dropped, anger threading through his words. "Those songs you're always singing are against the rules, too. Dad told you that."

As if she'd been singing something awful. Maddie's cheeks burned at the rebuke.

"You never obeyed Dad's rules. That's why he died." Noah dropped his head, shutting out everything, including Jesse's gentle explanation that there were many ways to worship God.

Maddie could see there was no use trying to reason with him. Noah had locked himself into his private world where rules controlled him and where no one else could enter.

"I'm sorry, but I think we'd better go home,"

she said to Jesse, and began packing up the picnic basket. "Thank you for a lovely evening. It was very kind of you to share your campsite with us."

She felt like crying as she urged Noah into the car. Tonight had been so wonderful, fun and carefree, almost like being a real family. Her heart ached for her son's pain and her own miserable past. Why couldn't they finally be free of Liam's rules?

"Thank you for coming." Jesse smiled, his demeanor absent of any chastisement or anger about their hurried exit. He bent his head to peer into the car at Noah in the backseat. "I'm glad you learned how to play a few notes," he said very quietly. "Playing my guitar is often the way I worship God when I can't think of the right words. Playing and singing something other than hymns isn't wrong. After all, King David made up his own songs. When he was a boy he played a lyre, which has strings kind of like a guitar. In the Bible it says he made up songs to sing to King Saul when he was upset."

"Really?" Noah's head lifted and his wide eyes fixed on Jesse's face.

Maddie felt her hurt and anger melt at the transformation she saw. Trust this wonderful man to know exactly how to reach her isolated son.

"When it comes to God, it all has to do with

your heart. That's what He looks at." Jesse tilted toward her and said in a voice too low for Noah to hear, "Don't look so worried, Maddie. Questions are a natural part of a kid's life. He's just trying to sort out the truth. You've done a good job with him. He'll figure it out."

Her heart burst into its own song of thanks for this wonderful man who'd come into their lives and changed both of them, helping them slowly break free of their darkened past. She should have climbed in her car and driven away. She should have said thank-you and let it go.

Maddie did neither. Instead she tilted forward on her tiptoes and pressed a kiss against Jesse's cheek. When she pulled back his blue eyes were wide with surprise.

"Thank you," she whispered.

"For what?"

"For being such a good friend to us." Then she did get in her car, and quickly drove away before she did or said something she would regret.

But all the way home she couldn't quite suppress the song her heart sang, a thank-you song to God, for Jesse Parker.

Chapter Seven

"No, Gran. Maddie didn't say a thing about that, but I'll check it out for you."

On Monday afternoon Jesse pocketed his phone with a frown as he waited for Tanner's signal to lead the horses into the ring where Noah's class waited. He'd already noted Maddie among the group of interested parents watching their kids from the sidelines. He'd tied his three horses to the rails, purposely spacing them so, hopefully, he'd end up next to her.

Gran was worried about issues at Quilt Essentials but at the moment Maddie seemed focused on Noah.

"Hi, Jesse." The welcome in her voice and that smile of hers made his stomach clench. Funny the effect she always had on him. "You look as weary as Tanner has since their new baby arrived."

"Nah. He looks worse." Jesse chuckled when she rolled her eyes. "It was nice of him to let me bring the puppies to Wranglers so I can maintain the feedings." He paused when Lefty pointed Noah toward a horse named Amos, which he guessed Tanner had chosen especially because it was so gentle. Thing was, Amos was not one of the horses Jesse was in charge of. "Your son looks terrified."

"He is. He can't seem to get comfortable around animals. Except the puppies, and that's only because you helped him." She bit her lip. "His teacher and I had to do some sweet-talking to get him to come here. She said several of the other children are also hesitant to take part."

"Today will help ease their fears. Excuse me." At Tanner's signal, Jesse nodded and stepped away to begin working with the kids and horses he'd been assigned.

His three students were knowledgeable about horses and required little guidance. But through the next few minutes he kept watch over Noah, and when it became clear that the wrangler helping him wasn't making progress and that Maddie was getting more worried by the moment, Jesse had a quick word with Tanner. A few minutes later he changed places with Noah's wrangler, who gave him a smile of relief.

"Two of the three are petrified," he muttered before walking away.

"What's wrong, Noah?" Jesse asked after fruitless attempts to get the boy to relax. A sideways glance showed Maddie's smile was returning. She had that much confidence in him?

Focus on your job!

"I don't want to ride this dumb old horse." Noah's bottom lip jutted out in a fashion that said he would not be persuaded otherwise.

"Oh." Jesse rubbed his chin. "How come?" He kept his tone even, conversational. "Would you rather have a different horse than Amos?"

"No." Noah averted his dark brown eyes. "I don't like horses," he said firmly.

"Because you're afraid of them?" Jesse guessed, in a quiet tone so his classmates couldn't overhear.

Noah inclined his head just slightly.

"But you come to Wranglers Ranch all the time and there are always horses here."

"I don't go near them. Dad's rule was to stay away from animals. Horses are dangerous." Noah crossed his arms over his thin chest protectively.

"They can be if you don't know how to treat them, but that's why you're here. To learn." Jesse prayed for wisdom to coax away Noah's fear. "In the Bible David said, 'When I am afraid I will put my trust in You.' That's a good thing to do, don't you think?"

"I guess." The boy didn't look convinced.

"I hope you'll at least try to ride Amos." Jesse employed his most pitiful tone.

"Why?" Noah frowned at him.

"Because if you don't he's going to be very disappointed."

"Horses don't get disappointed. They don't have feelings." Noah scoffed.

"Are you kidding me? Horses are very sensitive. Trust me, when the other horses get their treat for doing a good job here today and Amos doesn't get his, he'll be very disappointed." Jesse sighed and shook his head. "I sure don't like to see that, because Amos is such a good horse. He wants to do his job, but you won't let him."

Confused, Noah glanced from Jesse to his mother, who nodded encouragingly.

"Couldn't you at least try? Just so Amos can get a treat?" Jesse wheedled. "He's an old horse and he really loves his treats."

"Like s'mores?" Noah rolled his eyes.

"Nope. Horses can't eat chocolate." Jesse could see Noah was relenting, so he pretended nonchalance as he tilted back on his heels, stroked Amos's flank and pushed his point a little harder. "After this class each horse that works well gets half an apple and three carrots. Amos is real partial to apples. He can smell 'em from a long way away. Be a shame if he didn't get his apple, don't you think? But I guess if you're too scared to try…" He let that dangle.

"I don't want Amos to miss his apple." Noah glanced at the other kids. "I guess I could brush him like the others are doing."

"You could." Jesse pulled the currying tools out of a sack hanging over the rail. "Here you go. Nice and gentle, as if you were brushing your hair." He got Noah started, then turned to wink at Maddie, whose smile showed both concern and relief. "You're doing great," he praised, wondering why resurrecting Maddie's smile mattered so much.

His other two charges worked harmoniously, gibing each other as they groomed their mounts. All three kids seemed to grow increasingly more comfortable with their animals until Tanner blew his whistle signalling the end of that part of the lesson. Jesse could almost feel Noah's tension build.

"Don't worry," he murmured, resting his hand on the boy's shoulder. "We're just going to walk the horses around. So they get used to you." *And you to them.*

But when Noah didn't follow instructions, Jesse firmed up his directions.

"The rule is to lead your horse on the left side. Because it's the way Amos has learned, and doing things the same way makes it more comfortable for him," he added, forestalling the question forming on the boy's lips. "Keep Amos close to you and stay near his shoulder." He nodded when Noah stepped tentatively forward. "Good. But don't wrap the lead-rope around your wrist or arm. Hold it like this."

"He's too close." Noah jerked away, inadvertently tugging on the reins. Amos obligingly shifted sideways, which brought a yelp from the boy. "He's going to step on me!"

"No, he isn't. Listen to me, Noah." Jesse intervened, positioning himself between boy and animal. He crouched down to look into Noah's dark and fearful gaze. "Every horse learns the same set of rules. Amos knows all of them and he knows exactly what he's supposed to do when you pull on the reins. But if you don't follow the rules *he's* learned, he can't understand what you want. His rules are what tell him how he should behave."

"But—"

"You have to follow Amos's rules, Noah. Not yours." Jesse could see he wasn't making headway.

"It's the same as your rules, honey." Maddie's gentle voice from the sidelines brought calm to the tense atmosphere. "Your dad taught you not to lie. If he had suddenly asked you to lie, you'd be mixed up, wouldn't you? Because the rule you learned is no lying. This horse learned his horse rules and you have to follow them so you don't mix him up. Do you understand?"

Noah frowned, but his head jerked up and down.

"Listen to Jesse. If you do what he tells you, you'll be fine. You can trust him, Noah," she whispered. Her wide-eyed gaze locked with Jesse's.

So she trusted him? Around horses at least.

The rest of the lesson passed without incident, but Noah did not relax, nor did he become more comfortable with his horse, though Jesse's other pupils seemed to gain confidence. By the time they were finished, Jesse felt drained and ineffective. He was here to work with these kids, but wasn't succeeding. *Lord, how in the world do I help Noah?*

When the class ended everyone went to sample Sophie's cookies and juice, but Jesse stayed with the horses, leading them toward the barn as he pondered his failure.

"Noah didn't do very well, did he?" Maddie trailed behind him, her voice soft, almost apologetic. "I'm sorry. I know you tried."

"It will take time. Noah hasn't been around

animals that much." Jesse smiled at her. "He doesn't see them as much more than wild beasts."

"Liam's doing, I'm afraid." She walked beside him, her gaze on something distant. "He had this sermon he loved to preach about God giving subjugation of the animals to men. I used to wonder if perhaps..." Her voice died away.

"What?" Jesse's curiosity bloomed.

"Well, I wondered if he'd once been attacked and maybe become afraid," she murmured. "A parishioner offered to give Noah a puppy on his second birthday. Liam forbade it. He said God never meant for animals to be kept in a house."

So she'd bought the boy a dog for a Christmas gift hoping to normalize his childhood? Jesse handed over the horses to Lefty as he thought about that. He'd struggled hard to understand where Noah was coming from, yet he couldn't seem to get through to the boy. Again he considered asking Maddie to tell him more about Noah's father so he could figure out a way to counteract the kid's fears.

"Maybe you're right." He hesitated, then plunged ahead. "I'm really struggling to get a grip on what's going on in Noah's head, so I can help him enjoy the horses. Can you tell me anything else about your husband that might explain what he taught Noah?"

Maddie's face blanched. She gulped and blinked twice before clearing her throat. When she finally looked at him, Jesse was appalled by the dead look in her usually lively green eyes.

"Um, I don't know." There was a world of pain underlying that whispered response.

She's been through enough. Don't hurt her anymore, some voice inside his head ordered.

"Liam was very firm in his convictions." Her hesitant words warned Jesse that Maddie was about to say something important. "Sometimes that made him difficult to live with." She stared at the ground now, obviously feeling her way through a vortex of emotions. Then she lifted her head and looked directly at him. "I prayed all the time for God to help me be a good wife to Liam, but I wasn't. Why didn't God help me, Jesse?"

He couldn't answer. Not because he didn't know all the right words a minister should offer a hurting soul. Not because he couldn't cite a hundred verses that were often used to do just that. And not because her anguish didn't touch his heart.

Because it did. Deeply.

But Jesse felt that anything he said would only trivialize her pain. He understood her feelings of abandonment, had suffered them himself. He still searched for his own understanding of God's ways and hadn't yet found an answer that satisfied his questions.

But he had to say something. He owed her that much.

"I don't know why, Maddie." Feeling utterly ineffectual, he mouthed the one truth he still clung to. "All I know is that God cares for us with a love we can't fathom. What He does, He does for our good and for His kingdom. Keep talking to Him. That's what's most important."

Did the hope that had flared in those expressive eyes dim? Jesse chafed against his feelings of failure and vowed to spend more time seeking God's answers so he could help Maddie and Noah.

And himself.

"I'd better go. Noah will be leaving with his class and I need to get back to the store." Her words reminded him of his grandmother's earlier call.

"You have to work late again?" He already knew the answer, but he waited for her nod. "Why?"

"One of our employees was admitted to hospital last night for an emergency appendectomy. She was supposed to work this evening. I need to cover her shift." Maddie's tired face told him she was not looking forward to her extended workday.

"Is there no one you could hire to cover her absence?" Emma had spoken of someone named Talia, but Jesse wasn't going to suggest her. Maddie was the manager, and in Emma's absence, hiring decisions were up to her. He wanted her to feel confident, not undermined, and she would feel weakened if she learned Emma had called him.

"We have a couple of staff who work extra hours when we need them. I suppose I could contact one to cover, but it means changing the schedules, and I don't like to do that without Emma's approval. It might increase her expenses and change the benefit structure her bookkeeper has in place." Maddie sighed. "I haven't had time to speak with her personally about it so I think I'll just fill in until I can okay it with Emma."

Maddie nibbled on her bottom lip. It was something she did whenever she was unsure of herself, and though Jesse found it endearing, he also agreed with Emma's comment that this was a time for Maddie to make a managerial decision.

"Can I say something?" he began, praying for wisdom and the right words. "Gran is depending on you to run the store. And you're doing a terrific job. But what will happen if you take on too much, wear yourself out or get sick and can't be there for Emma? Who will keep Quilt Essentials going?"

"I never thought of that." She frowned and her shoulders slumped, as if she'd done something wrong.

"Gran once told me that the hardest thing she had to learn about running her business was learning to delegate. She said she started out very hands-on, managing every detail, until she realized that her staff needed to feel included. She said she finally realized that the best way to ensure a business's success is to make sure your employees feel like it's their business, too, so they will keep it operating when you can't be there." He waited, trying to gauge Maddie's reaction.

As she thought it through, her face slowly cleared of the worry and apprehension that had filled it. Finally, her sunny smile broke through.

"Thank you, Jesse. You always seem to have the answers I need." Maddie pulled out her new cell phone.

Too bad he didn't have the answers *he* needed.

"Hi, Talia. This is Maddie McGregor. I'm wondering if you can work this evening and cover Abby's shifts until further notice. She's in hospital. You can?" Her face blazed with joy. "Thank you so much. I know we haven't often worked together, but I hope we can get to know each other much better over the next few weeks." She closed the phone with a huge sigh.

"Sounds like you have tonight off," he said with a smile, and checked his watch. "I don't. It's puppy feeding time. Then I'll load them up and get home. Emma's roses need watering and weeding."

"Noah and I could help," she offered. "He talks a lot about the puppies. I think he is beginning to love them."

"I wouldn't turn down an offer of help." Nor an evening spent with Maddie.

Jesse knew he was going to have to refocus and stop involving himself in her life, but he owed it to Gran to help her friends where he could. Didn't he?

And as a Wranglers employee he had to do his best with Noah, too. Even if he didn't have a clue how to do that.

"It's really nice of you to make us dinner again, Jesse." Maddie loaded the dishwasher with the few dishes they'd used. "I never imagined it was so easy to make soup."

"It was nice of you and Noah to help with the puppies' feedings, weeding and watering Emma's rose garden, and with chopping vegetables," Jesse replied with a grin. "As long as you have vegetables you can always make soup."

He grimaced when Noah jumped three of his checkers and waited to be crowned.

"I'm good at this game." Noah's grin quickly faded. "But I'm not good with Amos." He turned his head to glance at her. "I shouldn't go to Wranglers Ranch with our class anymore. Right, Mom?"

"I don't know about that." Maddie pretended to think about it, wishing Jesse would jump in with some advice. But Noah was *her* son. It was up to her. "I don't think it's good to try something once and then quit. You need to give riding a fair chance."

"But I don't like it." He glowered at her.

"You didn't like the puppies at first, either," she reminded him quietly.

"Horses are different."

"Why?" She sat down at the table beside him, nursing her cup of tea.

"I dunno." Noah skipped his man across the board to win the game. "Do you want to play again?"

"No, thanks. Losing twice is enough." Jesse finished his own drink. "It's a gorgeous evening. Why don't we sit on Gran's deck?"

Maddie quelled a frisson of delight at the thought of spending more time with this man she admired so much.

"With your guitar?" Noah wore a hungry look.

"Yep. Is that okay?" he asked, pausing for Noah's nod before he lifted the instrument from its case.

Maddie thought it was very okay. She loved hearing Jesse's voice lift in the praise songs he favored.

"I guess." Noah followed them to the deck. He soon became riveted by Jesse's hand movements as he strummed the strings. The song that followed was a tender, poignant song of thanks to God for His wonderful goodness.

Maddie sat in stunned silence when Noah closed his eyes and let his head move to the rhythm of the music. Beat for beat her son's small fingers began to mimic Jesse's, sliding up and down the pretend neck of a guitar as if he, too, were playing. How could she have let Liam teach that worship such as this was wrong?

Maddie fell into her own meditation on the goodness of God, marveling at the sense of connection she'd only ever heard about but now glimpsed thanks to Jesse's music. His words voiced a complete confidence in God—a confidence that she didn't share.

But she yearned to. If only she could figure out how to find this sense of reverence when she was alone and feeling defeated...

"I guess that's enough for tonight," Jesse murmured some time later.

Feeling refreshed and renewed in spirit, Maddie blinked back to reality. Her glance at Noah showed that he, too, seemed less tense. Jesse's song had done that for both of them.

"I could feel the music," Noah exclaimed.

"Really? Show me." Jesse handed him the guitar.

After two false starts, Noah pursed his lips.

"Close your eyes now and try again," Jesse suggested.

Noah began again. In a jerky rhythm at first, but then evening out, her son reproduced the same haunting melody Jesse had played, but with a wistful edge. The night seemed to fall silent around them and even the stars seemed entranced by the boy's efforts. Maddie's heart squeezed with pride as he caressed the strings, coaxing every note until the last one died away into the darkness.

"That was wonderful, honey," she whispered, dashing away her tears because tears bothered him. Jesse had done this. For them. "So beautiful. How did you do it?"

"I dunno." Noah's face showed his own disbelief. "I just did what Jesse did and the song came."

"God's given you a gift for music, Noah," Jesse said, his voice filled with admiration. "I've never before met anyone who could pick up a tune after hearing it once or twice, let alone on an instrument they didn't know. You must develop your talent, practice and get better."

"Like it says on the barn at Wranglers, right?" Noah grinned. "Fan Into Flame the Gift That is Within You."

"Exactly." Jesse's gaze met Maddie's. "Each of us has a unique talent from God. Yours might be making music. I think your mom's gift is quilting and a heart for people."

It was so wonderful to be noticed, to be appreciated. What an amazing, caring man he was to take such an interest in them.

"Don't lock away your gift because of rules, Noah."

"You mean I should disobey my dad?" In a flash her son's expression changed to one of confusion. He glanced at Maddie with disapproval. "Like Mom did?"

"I don't think your dad knew you had this gift, Noah." A smile played across the former youth pastor's lips. "If he had I'm sure he would never have said what he did about music. I'm sure that if your dad knew that you could make the kind of worship music that helps people talk to God then he would want you to play it as often as you could. I think he'd understand and I think God understands about guitar music, too, because you're using it to praise Him and that's never wrong."

Frowning, Noah handed over the guitar. "I'm gonna feed the puppies again before we go home."

Maddie watched him leave the deck, her heart full of thanksgiving for the world that had been opened to him tonight.

"You're crying. Why?" Jesse murmured, taking the chair next to hers that Noah had vacated, and sliding his hand over hers.

"Because for the first time Noah's questioning his rules." Maddie was so moved she could hardly express herself. "Thanks to you."

"Don't get too excited." Jesse patted her hand and let it go but the warmth of his touch remained. "Kids are changeable. By tomorrow he'll probably revert to what's ingrained inside him. I think it's going to take a while for him to move beyond what's he's learned."

"You're probably right." The weight of parenthood settled heavily on her. Why had God let Liam, a minister, be so wrong? The same old question still had no answer, but just for tonight Maddie was going to cling to her faith that God was changing things for her and Noah. "I'd better get home. I have a big day tomorrow."

"Bigger than usual?" He gave her a questioning look when she nodded. "Why?"

"Emma's latest order of quilting supplies came in today. It's a lot of stuff and we've had a ton of requests for it all, so it will sell. But there are so many new items that I'll have to reorganize everything in the notions corner." She grimaced. "Even then I don't know if it will all fit."

"Couldn't you do a revolving thing like you did with that fabric?" he suggested.

"I'm not sure I know how that would work in such a small space, and I don't like to make too many changes without Emma's input," Maddie admitted.

"You're the manager. You'll think of a way to make the store work better." He grinned at her heavy sigh. "Maybe I could stop by tomorrow on my way home from work and help," he offered. "I'm on the early shift."

"That would be very kind, if you're sure you don't mind?" Why did her heart give this silly little hiccup at the thought of working with Jesse again?

"No problem." He seemed to hesitate.

"Was there something else?" she asked, curious about his silence.

"I was wondering if Noah could come back with me to Emma's after school sometimes." There was a hesitancy in his offer that she didn't understand. "Maybe he could help me with a few things."

"The dogs, you mean?"

"That and some ideas I have to make it easier for Gran to manage when she comes home. The steps up to this deck could be covered with a temporary ramp. That would make it easier for her to care for her roses. And maybe I can do something in her bathroom to simplify showering." Jesse was so thoughtful—about everyone. It was a trait Maddie greatly admired.

"Maybe Noah would enjoy helping you make Emma's home better. Let's ask him," she suggested, when he appeared. Jesse explained, then they waited for her son to decide.

"Okay, but…" Noah's eager look melted. "I dunno know how to build stuff."

"Well, of course you don't. You haven't learned. Yet." Jesse messed his hair, then laughed when Noah smoothed it. "We'll figure it out together."

"Tomorrow is swimming."

"You can't miss that," Jesse agreed. "Not when you're going to be a lifeguard." He grinned at Maddie. "So how about I pick up Noah, take him to his lesson and we come here after?"

"It's very kind of you. Thank you." She smiled at Noah. "We must get home now. Cocoa will want dinner."

"She's good at waiting," Noah said as they drove away. "I'm not."

Neither am I. Maddie chided herself for the excitement that thought brought her.

Funny how things seemed so much brighter with Jesse in the picture.

Chapter Eight

❧

"Very clever solution. I knew you were made for Gran's business." Jesse grinned.

After a month of continued contact over coffee, snacks and sometimes dinner, he'd fallen into an easy friendship with Maddie that revolved around Noah, Emma's prolonged recovery and both their jobs. Already Jesse saw many changes in the woman who sat across from him on the patio at Wranglers Ranch. For one thing she no longer shrank from every challenge but was slowly growing more confident in her ability to handle whatever came up.

"I doubt my new thread display is that crucial to the business," Maddie chuckled. "But thanks to your support and Emma's, too, I am learning that I can handle things. I couldn't ask for a better boss. Did you know she put me on an email list for a daily Bible study?"

Maddie's smile brought sunshine to Jesse's world and cheered his spirit, keeping him from dwelling on his perpetual 'Why, God?' questions.

"You're both really great encouragers."

"It's not so much us as it is you," he said quietly, studying the steam that floated upward from his coffee cup before he lifted his head to look into her lovely eyes. It wasn't that Maddie hadn't been poised before, but now she didn't raise her hand to cover her scar when he studied her. "You're beginning to understand that God didn't create dummies."

Her eyes flared wide before she burst out laughing.

"What's so funny?"

"You." She shook her head. "You wouldn't say that if you'd seen my macaroni and cheese dish last week." She wrinkled her nose and squeezed her eyes closed. "Disgusting."

"The one you made last night wasn't bad," he replied. Then, when her eyes demanded truth, he added, "Except for the charred parts."

Maddie hooted with laughter again, drawing Sophie's attention. The woman left Noah's school group and walked toward them. "More coffee?" she asked, holding the pot.

"Thanks, Sophie, but I'd better not. I need to get back to work." Maddie glanced at her son, her face pensive. "I only stopped by this morning to see how he's doing at riding." She pursed her lips. "Not that well apparently."

The baby monitor on Sophie's hip gave a wail and she hurriedly said goodbye before striding toward the house.

"Seeing Sophie with baby Carter almost makes me wish I could start over with Noah. I'd do things so differently, insist on a more normal childhood for one thing." She blinked again quickly. "He's growing away from me, Jesse. And I don't know what to do about it."

"Keep showing him you love him," her friend advised.

"I'm doing that, of course, but what if that's not enough?" Worry crowded out her smile. "He keeps pushing me away and I don't understand why."

"He's struggling internally." But with what, exactly? That was Jesse's conundrum. "My guess is that it has to do with his father's rules. Breaking them causes him a lot of self-doubt and pain. Something makes Noah feel he must keep them, or else. Only we don't know what the 'or else' is."

"Those stupid rules!" She modulated her voice when heads turned to study them. "I wonder if Liam had any idea of the problems his rules would cause."

"Did they cause problems for you when you were married?" Jesse hungered to know more details of Maddie's past and what had formed her into this amazingly strong woman.

"Yes, they caused problems for me." Her shoulders drooped. "I felt like I was in prison, that I couldn't be genuine. I had to become some caricature so that I fit all Liam's stipulations. Not that I ever knew who the real me was." She made a face. "I guess that's why working at Emma's was such a blessing. After our first meeting I was able to relax and enjoy my time with the fabrics and people. That meant a lot."

"And Liam didn't object?"

"I guess he thought I might as well earn some money, since I was hopeless at being a minister's wife." She shrugged. "I could only work while Noah was at school, but those precious hours were like my weekly vacation."

"Emma is blessed to have you." Jesse had noted several times that whenever her husband's name came up, Maddie tensed. "I know this might hurt you but I have to ask." He exhaled, then posed the question. "Is there some reason Noah might blame you for his dad's death?"

"Me?" She frowned, slowly shook her head. "Is that what he said? I can't imagine why."

"He didn't say it. Maybe I misunderstood. Forget it." Jesse brushed it off, not wanting to cause her any more distress. "His class is finished and the bus for the next one is pulling in. I'd better go." He swallowed the last of his coffee and rose. "Pray for me, will you, Maddie? My students in this group are really a challenge."

"Worse than Noah's class?" she teased.

"Noah's a piece of cake. A triangle-shaped piece." He grinned. How did this woman always manage to lighten his heart? "I could use a success story."

"Every child you work with is a success in the making, Jesse. Just be patient. God's on their case." She gave him a saucy grin. "It feels nice for *me* to encourage *you* for a change."

"I'll take all the encouragement you want to give," Jesse said, and meant it. He loved working on Wranglers Ranch, but his limited success with the kids was frustrating.

And yet, what else could he do? He could not, would not risk giving the wrong answers and being blamed for another tragedy, and he didn't know what else God wanted from him. It was like being in some kind of limbo.

"I promise I will pray for you. Now I must go." Maddie rose gracefully, her lovely green sundress a perfect foil for her dark hair and alabaster skin. "I'm going to try making spaghetti and meatballs tonight. Dare to join us?"

"Love to. It's my favorite."

"Apparently it's hard to burn. Or so the teacher says, although I'm not sure he knows just how skilled I am at doing that." She made a funny face, waggled her fingers, then walked toward her car.

Jesse watched her go with mixed emotions. That self-deprecating comment said a lot about Maddie. She was a very giving person, but she fought such a dark cloud of doubt. It sounded to him as if her husband had never praised her, never saw the wonderful woman she was. Liam McGregor must have been blind.

"See you after school, Jesse." Noah stood behind him, backpack in hand, ready to leave with his class.

"The puppies and I will be waiting as usual." Jesse grinned. "Bye." He watched Noah leave, a solitary figure, head bent, eyes fixed downward.

Why can't I help him, Lord? his heart asked, as the same old feelings of helplessness welled. *Show me what You want me to do.*

Maybe God was busy today, because Jesse wasn't struck with any ideas, and he had little success relating to the rest of his charges. The second lesson of the day ended with him feeling utterly frustrated. These kids needed him and he wanted so desperately to ask and probe and find out what was bothering them and try to help. Yet he was afraid lest he give the wrong response and cause irreparable harm.

Afraid? He'd never felt that so strongly before and he didn't like the sense of helplessness it provoked.

Jesse was also a bit envious of Maddie's progress in her spiritual journey. She was beginning to bloom, slowly gaining confidence in herself, figuring out her personal worth, while he couldn't find the niche where he belonged. Counseling, encouraging, mentoring—it was what he wanted to do, what he *needed* to do. But how to do it without messing up?

Jesse heaved a sigh. God knew he wanted to serve, but he was also leery about getting too involved. Why didn't He reveal how Jesse could get past that? Frustrated, he got busy cleaning and storing tackle until Tanner called his name.

"That redheaded kid in Noah's class that you were working with? Kendal? What are your thoughts on him?" the rancher asked.

"Off the cuff?" Jesse waited for Tanner's nod. "He's bored and spoiled. There are too many people in his world devoting too much time to him and he couldn't care less. He's a bully and his curiosity about horses is less than minimal," he said honestly.

"Blunt and not flattering, but I agree. That's why it seemed odd when I overheard him getting a stern lecture from Noah about handling the puppies gently." Tanner scratched his chin, then shoved back his Stetson. "And Kendal took it, probably because Noah wouldn't allow him to touch them unless he did it without hurting them." Tanner grinned. "Bit of an eye opener about both of them, don't you think?"

"Never thought Kendal would take directions from anyone." Jesse frowned. "Never thought Noah would give them either."

"Be interesting to see what comes of that relationship." Tanner nodded and walked away.

Jesse completed the rest of his work with his thoughts on Maddie's son. Music and puppies; those were Noah's interests. They seemed to give him a sense of accomplishment and belonging. Apparently Kendal liked the puppies. Could music reach him, too?

As Jesse waited for Noah to arrive from school, ideas began to bloom, ways to engage the kids who came here because they sought something to make them feel better about themselves.

Is that what I'm here to do?

Fanciful ideas filled his mind. Jesse wasn't totally sure if it was God's or his own interests that prompted them. Either way, he was intrigued. It wasn't the ministry he'd had before, but at least he would be doing something for these kids. Maybe then he wouldn't feel so... useless?

"You want to start a Wranglers Ranch band?" Maddie wasn't sure she understood what Jesse was proposing, but she wanted to hear more.

"I think I do." After a very good spaghetti dinner, Jesse walked beside her through the desert near her home, appreciating its tranquil beauty in the twilight.

Noah stayed ahead, checking out the profusion of cactus blooms. When he did speak it was to Jesse. He gave only monosyllabic answers to Maddie's conversation, and she struggled to crush the building fear that she was losing him.

Stop being afraid. God didn't make you a mother to take away your needy son. He wants you to help Noah grow. At least, that's what Emma's email had advised this morning.

"But how and what will a band do for the kids?" Remembering how Noah had been touched by Jesse's music increased Maddie's curiosity.

"I'm not sure. The idea is still in the germination stage. But I've seen music reach into a heart when nothing else could." Jesse's introspective voice was so quiet she had to lean near to hear it.

"Okay, so a band. Instruments?" Her brain immediately skipped to ways to make his idea happen.

"I don't know." Jesse sounded tense. "I don't know how it would work. Anyway, Tanner would have to approve the plan first."

"I don't think Tanner's approval will be a problem. He's all for anything that will help Wranglers Ranch reach kids." She paused, halted him with a hand on his arm, and when he looked at her questioningly, asked, "What's really bothering you, Jesse?"

"I'm a youth pastor, Maddie. I am—at least I thought I was—supposed to minister to kids."

"And a band isn't a ministry?" she challenged, then softly murmured, "Or is it a ministry you don't want? Maybe you feel it's not on the same level as being a youth leader."

He frowned at her so fiercely that she wondered for a moment if she should retract her comment.

"You're calling me a snob." Jesse didn't look pleased, but he didn't immediately dismiss the notion, either. He threaded his fingers in hers and gently pulled so she'd resume their walk. "Maybe I am, but it's because I never had any doubts that youth ministry was where God wanted me. Then Scott died and, well, nothing makes sense anymore."

"Working at Wranglers Ranch is working with youth," Maddie reminded him, loving the warmth of his palm against hers.

"I know, but—" he glanced sideways at her "—I never thought of it as permanent. It's only a stopgap until I figure out where God wants me."

"Maybe the band idea is His way of showing you." She waited as he digested that possibility, letting her mind explore her own new idea. "Maybe He's showing me something, too."

"You've got that look," Jesse said, following Noah's lead along the path, which arced back toward her home.

"What look?" She met his gaze and blushed at the familiarity she saw there. Jesse was *such* a good friend. "You're not the only one who gets ideas."

"That's what scares me." He pretended fear. "It's not more shelving, is it?"

Maddie could no more have stopped her burst of laughter than she could squelch the spurt of joy that bubbled inside as she returned his grin. In front of them Noah turned to see what was going on. His gaze slid from their faces to their clasped hands. Immediately a frown tipped the corners of his mouth down, his disapproval obvious. Was that why she yanked her hand from Jesse's? Noah turned and walked on.

"It is shelves, isn't it?" Jesse sighed.

"No more shelving," she promised. "This is something different. I want Quilt Essentials to try something only I'm scared to tell Emma."

"Nobody is ever scared of my marshmallow-hearted grandmother." He frowned at her sober look. "What's this idea, Maddie?"

"There's a nursing home around the corner from the store." The idea grew clearer as she continued. "I met the administrator at church last Sunday and she told me that she missed Emma's weekly visits. Apparently, many of your gran's former quilting buddies are now in that home. The administrator said those ladies talk all the time about the quilting bees they used to hold, about their fond memories of sitting around a quilt frame, chatting as they worked together stitching. The administrator thinks it would lift their spirits tremendously if they had something like a quilting party to look forward to each week. But her staff don't have the time or knowledge to be in charge of such a project."

"And so Maddie McGregor, being the softie she is, came up with a plan." He chuckled at her glare. "You're just like Gran, you know. She told me you've taken over most of her charity projects, improved on a lot of them, especially the community garden for inner city kids." His eyes gleamed with unspoken support. "Gutsy move, lady, and very generous."

"My grandmother and I used to work in her garden together. It's no big deal," she demurred.

"It's a big deal for someone who used to be afraid of her own shadow," he teased. "Your confidence is growing and it's wonderful to see. Now tell me your plan and how I can help."

She loved his immediate offer of help without all the 'have you thought of this' and 'what about that' questions with which Liam had always squelched her ideas. Jesse trusted her knowledge and gave her credit for being able to think through her plan. Just another thing to admire about Jesse Parker.

"The goal is to get those ladies quilting. I can put together a quilt top for them to sew, but I'd need to get a frame to the home and set it up with the top, bottom and batting. Doable. But the biggest thing is, one of our staff would have to be present, at least for the first few meetings." She waited, and when he didn't speak, added, "That's going to increase the payroll."

"Well, yes, but it's also going to provide some good publicity while benefiting some lonely ladies. I say go for it."

Jesse's support was a boost to her confidence, but still Maddie hesitated. "It could turn out to be a flop," she warned. "And to do it without consulting Emma—"

"But Gran told me that as far as operations go, she wants you to go with your hunches, so she can concentrate on her recovery." Jesse's words made Maddie wonder how much he'd discussed her with Emma.

"Yes, but this isn't the same as her other projects."

"Of course it is." Jesse sounded impatient. "By now you know of the many things Emma does for the community, so you know they're not all done for profit. My grandmother genuinely cares about people." He brushed her cheek with his knuckles. "You have the same heart for people that she does, Maddie. So go with what your heart is telling you." His blue eyes softened and his voice dropped as he said, "Forget the past, forget Liam and his rules. Listen to the faith that tells you God is there, ready and waiting to guide and help you."

"I never thought of God waiting to help me personally. I guess I don't have the same faith that you do," she admitted in a low voice, so Noah wouldn't hear.

"Are you kidding me?" Jesse gaped. "You had the faith to start the Easter quilt and believe your students would finish on time. You had the faith to start new projects, renovate the store, take cooking lessons and keep raising your son while filling in at Gran's community projects. Are you telling me you're not trusting God to help you with each of those things?"

"I guess," she said, slightly shocked to realize it was true. "I *have* been praying about a way to help those friends of Emma's."

"Now you've got your answer." God answering prayer was so ordinary to Jesse, but Maddie couldn't quite believe He'd do that for her.

"Can I ask you something?" She deliberately stopped a short distance from the house. Noah was sitting on the deck, playing with Cocoa for a change.

Jesse had helped them in so many ways. Could he help her with this?

"Ask anything." He studied her face as he waited.

"How do you know if you're good enough for God?" Seeing his confusion, she reworded it. "How can you tell if you qualify for God's love?"

"Everybody qualifies." He tilted his head to one side. "I'm not sure I understand."

"Well…" Maddie felt foolish, and yet she needed to know. "I wasn't a very good wife." Jesse's frown only added to her discomfort so she finally blurted, "I don't think I loved Liam the way I was supposed to. I don't think I'm a very good mother, either, because it seems like Noah hates me. So how can God love me?"

"God's love doesn't depend on what you do or feel." Jesse studied her with an intensity that made her shift nervously. "God loves you, Maddie McGregor, because God is love. He created every single thing about you, from your gorgeous hair to your beautiful eyes to your wonderfully talented hands. So He doesn't think *Oh, this child of mine is worth loving, but this one is too bad or too silly or too dumb.* He knows exactly who and what we are and He loves us anyway."

"I don't understand that," she admitted sadly.

"Sure you do." He jerked a thumb over one shoulder. "When Noah was born did you think *How can I love this wrinkled, red-faced, squalling kid that smells?*" He laughed at her frown. "Of course you didn't. You didn't ask how or why you loved him or how he was going to earn your love. You looked at him and thought, *This is my precious boy and I love him.* Am I right?"

"Yes." She glanced at Noah and felt the same rush of love she'd felt the day he was born.

"So if you can feel that way about your child, don't you think the God of the universe who created us can feel the same love for us, only infinitely stronger?" His smile, calm, certain and so kind, reassured her. "See, Maddie, it's not about who we are. It's about who He is. And He is love."

"So it doesn't matter what I do?" she asked, still confused.

"Of course it matters. But what you do won't change whether or not He loves you. Malachi 3:6 says, 'I the Lord do not change.' James 1:17 says, 'Every good and perfect gift coming down from the Father of the heavenly lights who does not change like shifting shadows.' And of course you know John 3:16. 'For God so loved the world,'" Jesse began, then paused, one eyebrow arched, waiting for her to finish quoting the verse.

When she'd said the rest, Maddie began slowly walking again, her brain busy with all she'd heard.

"The best way to show our love for God is to trust that because He loves us, He will always do His best for us. Ask God for help when you need it, Maddie, and then believe He's there with you, leading you through the hard parts." Jesse's voice lowered as they neared Noah. "Remember, God is love. It has nothing to do with rules or payback or anything else."

"Thank you." Feeling as though a huge weight had slid off her shoulders, Maddie was able to smile at Noah even though he was glaring at her. "Something wrong, son?"

"What were you whispering about?" he demanded, his tone argumentative.

"God," Jesse said, before she could respond. "And His love for us."

"Dad said people talk about love too much. He said they should talk less and do more." Noah's chin thrust up as he stared down the youth pastor with a hint of belligerence.

Maddie bit her bottom lip at the jaded comment, but Jesse was nodding.

"That may be true, Noah. Many people do talk about love more than they actually love." He smiled, then shrugged. "But the thing is, if you don't tell someone you love them, how would they know? And if you don't keep saying it, they might believe you stopped. So it's good to talk about love and to be loving, too. Don't you think so?"

Noah frowned, obviously thinking about it. "I guess," he muttered.

"I'd better get home. Puppy time." Jesse made a face.

"Haven't you been able to cut down on their feedings?" Maddie asked curiously.

"Oh, yeah, but I've also learned that if I give them a good solid feed right before bedtime, they almost make it through the night and I get a longer sleep." Jesse's smug grin made her laugh.

"So no guitar tonight?" Noah sounded disappointed.

"Some other time maybe." Jesse smiled at him. "You should get your own guitar. Then you could play whenever you want. Thanks for dinner. Bye." He left a few minutes later.

After Noah was in bed, his face turned to the wall when she tried to kiss him good-night, Maddie found her favorite spot on her porch and fought to quell the hurt that burned inside while wondering what she'd done wrong. Jesse had said God knew her. But did she know Him?

As she watched the stars twinkle in the night sky, her mind tried to fathom God. He knew the solar system. He knew every single star, even the ones scientists were still discovering. He knew what was wrong with Noah. He knew her.

Which meant He also knew about the fondness growing in her heart for the only man she'd ever called friend. He knew how much she appreciated Jesse's encouragement, his support, his steady assurance that she could be and do the things she'd dreamed of. God knew how she spent her day dreaming about when she'd see Jesse again and share her day with him, how she valued the way he built her up instead of crushing her hopes.

So God must know Maddie no longer thought of the future without Jesse in it. He must know she was falling in love with this wonderful man. He certainly knew that Jesse was a man worth loving.

But God also knew she was afraid to be vulnerable to love again. She'd raced into marriage with Liam to escape her father, had trusted too easily and gullibly believed that because Liam was a minister he would be a good husband. She'd been so wrong, made so many mistakes, chief among them that she hadn't loved her husband as she should have.

Jesse was nothing like Liam, of course, but she didn't know him that well, either. She didn't know his plans for the future or how he thought of her beyond friendship. She sure didn't know whether he shared this breathless feeling whenever they were together. She couldn't tell if he wanted to hold her hand as much as she loved him holding it, or whether he wanted to deepen their friendship as much as she did.

Once, Maddie had made a horrible mistake about love. She was not going to make it again.

"Show me how to be content with the precious time we spend together," she murmured. "I've made so many mistakes, done so many dumb things. I don't deserve to be loved either by You or someone as kind as Jesse. I know that. So help me be his very best friend. Help me help him find what You need him to see so he can be the pastor you want."

She sat long into the darkness, trying to think of a way she could help, but couldn't come up with a thing. But she wasn't going to give up. Somehow she would help him though because Jesse was worth caring about.

Chapter Nine

"You're not really into this, are you?" Kendal met Jesse's blink of surprise with a smirk. "I mean, helping us poor unfortunate dummies who don't know how to ride a horse—it's not really your favorite job."

"Why do you say that?" Stunned by the confrontation, Jesse swallowed, then did his job by pointing to the reins the boy had let dangle.

"Doesn't seem like you're here with us." Kendal picked up the reins. "You recite directions in a computer-type voice, like you don't care about us. You're just doing what they told you to do. We don't really matter to you."

Jesse opened his mouth to deny the accusation, but then he saw Noah watching and couldn't do it. Hadn't Tanner been working overtime to teach these kids truth? How could he slough off Kendal's indictment when it *was* the truth? He'd refused to allow himself to be engaged on a personal level so he *was* a fake, and kids could spot fakes a mile out, especially a whip-smart kid like Kendal.

What kind of emissary for God are you? Shame filled Jesse.

"You're right, Kendal. I wasn't here. I was thinking about something else. I'm sorry, guys. You now have my full attention. Let's get ready for your lesson." Jesse waited for the boys' nods. At his behest, Kendal finished checking that his saddle was secure on his horse. "Good work. Now can you get up on your own?"

"Sure." Kendal vaulted onto the horse, settled into the saddle, then peered down at him. "What were you thinking about?"

About to make some bland comment, Jesse caught the way Kendal glanced at Noah, as if to say, *Wait for it. He'll make something up.*

Jesse inhaled. "I've been thinking about starting a band, only I can't decide if anybody'd be interested." Let's see what the kid made of that honest response.

Kendal's usually bored stare snapped to life. "What kind of a band?"

"A kids' band. A Wranglers Ranch band." He glanced at Noah, who was making no effort to get on his horse. "Noah's interested in the guitar, I think, but I don't know if any other kids who come here can play an instrument. Maybe nobody wants to. Anyway, sorry. I should have been paying more attention to you guys."

"You didn't tell me you play the guitar." Kendal studied Noah with awe in his eyes.

"I'm just learning." Noah sounded panicked.

"He's good." Jesse kept talking as he maneuvered Amos so the stirrup was right in front of Noah. "He picks up a tune like nobody's business and he's hardly ever touched a guitar before." He kept heaping on praise as he lifted an unsuspecting Noah into the saddle.

"Jesse, I, uh, I don't like this." Noah sat stiffly, worriedly scanning the ground below.

"Hey, Noah? Can you show me how to play sometime?" Kendal nudged his horse to fall into the line of horses slowly plodding along.

"I dunno." Noah bobbled wildly on Amos, who knew exactly what was expected of him and followed the others around the ring.

He didn't say no.

"Anybody can learn an instrument." Jesse was secretly delighted that Noah didn't try to slide off the horse. Not that the boy was exactly participating. He sat stiffly, face frozen. "The thing is, it couldn't be a once-in-a-while thing. If you're in a band you have to be there for every practice and you have to work together. Bands take teamwork."

Tanner led the group through a walk and into a trot. Noah bounced wildly, clinging in terror to Amos's mane. When the horse moved into a slow canter, Noah rocked so violently Jesse grew concerned he would topple off so he jogged alongside.

"Don't pull on the reins like that," he said, and adjusted them. "You have to sit *in* the saddle, not on it. Keep your back straight. That's better. Relax, buddy. Amos knows what he's doing." He ran beside Amos, giving directions to both boys. Kendal quickly caught on, but Noah clung to his fear.

"I can't do it," he gasped, when they slowed to a walk.

"You can't if you keep being afraid." Jesse stopped him long enough to adjust his stirrups. "You have to think of Amos as part of you. You move with him by letting your hips shift, not by yanking on the reins or grabbing the saddle horn or bouncing around like a sack of potatoes. Ready to try again?"

"It's scary, Jesse." Noah's face lost all color as he gulped.

"It's only scary because you're not moving with your horse." He waited for a smile, but none was forthcoming. A flicker of inspiration flared. "There aren't always rules to guide you through the hard parts in life, Noah. Sometimes you just have to trust."

Two more rounds in the ring and Jesse was ready to give up, as feelings of failure engulfed him. Why couldn't he help Noah let go of his anxiety?

And then Kendal yelled, "If you can play a guitar you can ride that old horse, Noah."

Noah's smile barely flickered, but it was the signal Jesse needed.

"Close your eyes."

"Wh-what?" Noah looked at him as if he was crazy.

"Close your eyes and feel Amos moving, just like you felt the guitar music. Close them. Now!"

Noah glared at him, but finally squeezed his eyes shut, though his whole body was rigid with fear. With a touch, Jesse nudged Amos forward, holding his breath as the horse began to canter.

"Feel what Amos is doing," he ordered, but Noah seemed frozen. "*Feel* it." He waited, whispering a prayer.

And then something wondrous happened. Noah began to move with the horse, using his back and legs to control his movements instead of his hands. It took only a few minutes before he and Amos were smoothly circling the ring, horse and rider as one.

"Yes!" Jesse whispered, and fist-pumped to celebrate. He caught Tanner's grin and returned it.

"Way to go, Noah," Kendal cheered.

Noah opened his eyes, looking dazed but supremely happy. "I did it," he said with wonder as he reined in the horse.

"You sure did. That was perfect."

Jesse stood ready lest Noah freeze up again. Instead the boy nudged Amos's sides and directed him toward his spot at the rail.

"Very good work, guys. Both of you deserve those cookies today."

"And Amos?" Noah dismounted and stood studying the big animal. Then without warning he reached out and placed his hand flat against the horse's flank. "Will he get his treat?"

"Check my back pocket. I've got two sugar lumps there. You and Kendal each take one. Put it in your palm and hold it out. Your horses will take it from you." Seeing those dark eyes cloud again, Jesse touched the boy's shoulder. "Trust, Noah."

With a nod Noah looked at Kendal and together they held out their sugar lumps. Their horses delicately swooped up the treats, and then Amos nudged his head against Noah's, making the boy's dark eyes widen.

"That's how he says thank-you," Jesse explained with a chuckle.

"Oh." Noah nodded. "You're welcome, Amos. Thanks, Jesse." With a grin tossed over one shoulder, Noah headed toward the patio with Kendal, the two chatting like magpies.

"I don't know how you did that." Maddie stood under a palo verde tree, tears streaming down her cheeks. "But thank you, Jesse. Thank you so much."

"I didn't know you were here." He pulled a tissue out of his pocket and handed it to her. "You better mop up those tears before Noah sees you. He'd be embarrassed to have his mom bawling with his new friend watching."

"He rode a horse and made a friend—a kid who's terrified of horses and doesn't make friends." Maggie's sunny smile peeked out as the hand holding the tissue waved in the air. "You did that, Jesse Parker. You. I'm so glad God sent you here especially for Noah. Thank you."

And then, before Jesse could say or do a thing, Maddie McGregor slipped between the fence rails, threw herself into his arms and pressed a kiss against his cheek. One of Jesse's hands held the horses' reins, but as if of its own volition the other wrapped around her narrow waist, drawing her close. His senses burst to life at the fragrance of lilies that always surrounded Maddie.

When her lips brushed his, his heart rate surged into the danger zone. How could he help but return her kiss? He couldn't. So he kissed her back, wishing it would go on forever—until a snicker behind him made him pull away. He turned to see Lefty grinning at them.

"I'll look after these fellas, Jesse," he said, his eyes twinkling as he gathered the horses' reins. "You just, uh, get on with what you were doing."

"Thanks." It was then Jesse realized that all the hands were watching them, smirks on every face. Funny, but he didn't care a hoot. Not if it meant getting kissed by Maddie. Still, he'd prefer to do that in private. "Have you got time for coffee?" he asked her.

"A quick one. I used my lunch hour to come here." She walked with him toward the main house. "Emma phoned. Apparently she's to be released the day before Palm Sunday. She wants to know if we can pick her up then."

"In three weeks? Seems a bit early to me." As he walked with her to the patio, Jesse forced himself to stop reliving that kiss. He fetched them both coffee and cookies, liking that Maddie chose a table away from the others that offered a modicum of privacy. Truth was, he liked an awful lot about this woman.

"She'll be home for Easter." Maddie sipped her coffee thoughtfully. "I think we should have the puppies gone before she comes home. They're getting so active. The last thing she needs is to trip over one."

"I've been working on that," he told her, loving the way she immediately thought of his gran's welfare. Maddie and her generous heart. "So far I've found homes for four of them. Five more to go."

"Good." Only Maddie didn't look that happy about the departure of the pups, and he knew why. She'd grown very fond of them. As had they all.

"My parents will probably visit Gran for Easter," he mused, then explained, "Easter was always a really big celebration in our house."

"Oh." Maddie look puzzled by that which made Jesse think her husband had probably overseen very solemn Easters, missing out on the precious joy of that blessed event.

"One reason is that when you live in Colorado, Easter signals spring and the end to winter and cold." He shivered, then grinned. "But mostly I loved Easter because in our church it was a whole weekend of celebrating Christ's death and His rising from the grave. Potlucks, great services, youth get-togethers and the most joyful music ever created. Easter is still my favorite time of the year."

They were interrupted by Kendal and Noah.

"Can me and Noah be in that band?" Kendal asked. "I used to take saxophone lessons and I got pretty good." His boast deflated when Jesse studied him. "Least, I can play. Some of the other kids in our class play other stuff, too. You should ask them to join."

Jesse glanced at Maddie, who smiled encouragement at him. He took the plunge.

"Okay, but Tanner says you have to have a permission slip from your parents or guardians. And I say you have to be here every Monday and Wednesday after school for practice. You can ask others if they want to join. We'll hold a meeting about it after class on Friday. That's when we'll decide if we have enough people to start Wranglers Ranch Band."

Kendal squealed, high-fived Noah, then at the honk on the bus's horn, dragged him toward it, pausing only in his chattering to announce the band start-up to every kid they passed.

"You've certainly got them excited. Even Noah." She checked her watch, frowned, then studied him. "Jesse, can I ask another favor? Don't worry, it's not for Quilt Essentials. It's for Noah. I want to buy him a guitar, but I don't know anything about them. Would you—"

"I'll be happy to help you with that. When?" Privately, Jesse hoped getting a guitar might diffuse some of the anger the kid directed at his mother, frosty glares Maddie pretended not to notice but which always dimmed the light in her lovely eyes.

"Can we go today? After school?" Her face tightened for a moment before she gulped and shook her head as if to rid herself of anything negative. "Lately Noah barely speaks to me. I'm at a loss to figure out what's wrong, but maybe a guitar will help."

"Don't worry, he'll come around, Maddie. Just keep praying and trusting God," Jesse, urged, then wondered how he could give that advice when he couldn't seem to take it himself.

"I'm trying. I'm trusting you, too, Jesse. If anyone can reach Noah, you can. You already have." She wore the same wide smile he'd seen earlier when she'd embraced him. "I appreciate you so much."

"I appreciate you, too, Maddie." He fought an overwhelming urge to hug her, to kiss away the tiny furrow of worry on her forehead when her gaze lingered on Noah's departing bus. "Especially the things you've done for Emma. Organizing that bus trip for her friends to visit her this week was very thoughtful and gracious of you."

"She sounded a little down, so I thought maybe a visit from familiar faces would help." Maddie frowned as she walked toward her vehicle. "I wish I'd been able to go with you to visit her last weekend, but it's been so crazy busy at the store. Still, I feel guilty—"

"No guilt." He tapped a forefinger against her lips. "Gran knows you're juggling a bunch of different balls. Truthfully, I think knowing you're right here to handle anything that Quilt Essentials needs has freed her to concentrate on her recuperation."

"I'm happy to help. She was my lifeline when—" Maddie pretended to cough, covering whatever she'd been about to say. When she resumed speaking she changed the subject. "So see you after school?"

"Yes. I'll bring Noah to the store and we'll go guitar shopping from there." He hated the worry lingering in the back of her eyes. She did so much for everyone else. *Please help heal her past and her relationship with Noah,* Jesse prayed.

With a swirl of emotions, he watched Maddie drive away. She was gorgeous inside and out. She gave unstintingly, without being asked, and she always made time for people. She was living the Christian life he espoused. Maddie McGregor was exactly the kind of generous, giving woman he'd once imagined would share his ministry. He knew he could count on her to be in his corner as she had been today, cheering him on, praising his efforts, encouraging him with her gentle soul that asked so little in return.

Jesse cared a lot for Maddie.

That realization stunned him for a moment. But then he pulled himself back to reality. He no longer had a ministry to share with her. He was a simple ranch hand who was as scared to risk himself with kids as Noah had been to ride a horse.

Except that Noah had got over it.

Shoving away those guilty feelings Jesse wondered; even if he let this attraction for Maddie proceed, what could he offer her? He had no ministry, no special call on his life. Not anymore. In fact, the brutal truth was that he secretly feared God had abandoned the call that Jesse had heard so long ago. Even if by God's grace he was given a new one, what if he messed up again? Would he shame and embarrass Maddie so badly that she'd dump him, as Eve had?

His brain told him no, but his heart burned as he imagined the devastation he'd feel if Maddie ever looked at him in disgust. He tried to envision his world if she wasn't there in his life every day, if he couldn't see her sweet smile nudging him to keep pushing on, if she didn't surprise him with a kiss or a half-burned meal or some new idea for the store that needed his help.

Maddie was moving beyond her painful past and learning to grow in God, to explore who He had created her to be as she lived out her faith. Jesse knew it wasn't easy for her, but she faced each obstacle, testing her newfound faith while expecting God to help.

If Maddie and Noah could trust God, why couldn't Jesse do the same?

She'd kissed Jesse!

Maddie spent the rest of the morning and part of the afternoon alternately appalled by her behavior and reliving the glory of those few blissful moments in Jesse's arms. It had felt so right to be there, to show him how much he meant to her. She'd ached to tell him she loved him.

And yet he'd said nothing about caring for her.

"I think you'll find adding the fabrics in these fat eighths will give a spectacular heritage look to your quilt," she told her customer as she tied a pretty blue bow to the handles of a white paper bag with Quilt Essentials embossed on it. "Enjoy."

"I will. Thank you." The woman hurried away, a smile on her face.

"Do all your customers leave looking so happy?" A smiling Jesse stood in front of the counter with Noah at his side.

"I hope so. Hi, Noah. Did Jesse tell you what we're doing this afternoon?" She glanced from her sulky son to Jesse and immediately her heart began that silly dance of joy. Just seeing him made her happy.

When Noah shook his head, she said, "We thought we'd go shopping for a guitar. That's if you're still interested in joining Jesse's band?"

"Yeah. Me and Kendal are joining." Noah's eyes widened as he gazed at Jesse. "Thank you."

"It was your mother's idea," Jesse told him, but to Maddie's extreme disappointment he ignored that and began peppering his mentor with a ton of questions that continued on the drive to the music store.

Once there Maddie again felt shut out as Noah walked through the store, more excited than she'd seen him for years. But it was Jesse he turned to, Jesse's opinion he sought, Jesse who received his thanks and praise.

Heart aching, Maddie told herself to ignore it. He was excited, that's all. He'd include her later. But even when, with Jesse's help, Noah finally settled on the guitar he wanted, even after she'd paid for it and they were on their way back to the store to retrieve Jesse's truck, Noah barely spoke to her. And then only to say thanks in a quick, abrupt way, because Jesse told him to.

This is so hard, God.

"You're welcome, Noah. I hope you have many years of enjoyment from it." Keeping her smile in place, she endured the searching look he gave her before he turned back to Jesse.

They drove to Emma's because Jesse wanted her help to choose the right pup to give to one of her staff at Quilt Essentials. They sat in Emma's backyard sharing a coffee and laughing together while Noah tried to tie a ribbon around the chosen pup's neck. But Maddie couldn't completely disguise the pain she felt when her son ignored her. Jesse, being who he was, saw that and offered some comfort. She loved him for it.

"He's going through a phase, Maddie. He'll get over it. Don't let it get to you. Just keep clinging to God." He slid an arm around her shoulder and squeezed as if to impart his strength to her.

"I'm trying, but it's not easy." She gulped to stem her tears. "I don't understand what I've done to make him so angry."

"It isn't you," Jesse assured her. "It's him. He's got a battle going on inside. I promise I'll try and help him figure it out."

"You're such a good friend." She gazed into his eyes. Didn't he feel anything more than friendship for her? "Thank you, Jesse."

"My pleasure." He checked his watch and rose, holding out a hand to help her up. "We'd better get that pup to the store before his new owner finishes her shift."

"Yes." Sad to end this time of sharing by giving away one of the animals that had brought and kept them together, Maddie grasped his hand and stood, noticing Noah's fierce frown as he studied the two of them and their joined hands. "Why don't you and Noah do that while I go home and start dinner? You're welcome to join us if you want to risk it," she said, hoping desperately that he would. She wasn't sure how much more of Noah's angry silence she could endure.

"What's on the menu for tonight?" Jesse asked keeping his expression bland.

"I have one more meal to make before Friday's class. Lasagna. I assembled everything this morning, so all I have to do is put it in the oven and make a salad." She frowned. "I think I did it right, but it will take an hour or so to cook, the recipe says."

"Good. That's just enough time for Noah and me to run our errand and then take Cocoa for a walk." Jesse winked at her. She knew he was trying to tell her he'd use the time to sound out her son.

"Sounds good." She dusted off her skirt. Tears

welled as she picked up the puppy and brushed
a kiss against its sweet nose. "Bye, sweetie."

"He's going to a good home." Jesse's whispered reassurance comforted her.

"I know." She handed the dog to Noah then
touched his cheek, trying to remain impassive
when he jerked away. "See you later, guys."

"You will," Jesse promised.

On the drive home and while she worked in
the kitchen, Maddie sent up a steady barrage of
prayer for help, understanding and wisdom. As
she sat on the porch watching Jesse and Noah
wander through her patch of desert, she whispered a second prayer.

"I love Jesse so much, God. Isn't there a way
he could be more than just a friend? Could you
make him love me?"

But after dinner, when Jesse had left and the
sun was setting, doubt swept in. Emma's Bible
study said that when you prayed for something,
you were supposed to ask God with confidence
that He would answer. Only Maddie didn't feel
confident asking for Jesse's love. The Bible said
wives were supposed to love their husbands.
Liam had quoted the verses constantly to remind her of her duty.

Yet no matter how hard she'd tried, Maddie hadn't loved him. She'd disobeyed God's

laws. How could she expect Him to trust her—a woman who'd blown her first marriage—with the love of a wonderful man like Jesse?

Chapter Ten

❧

"What a gorgeous day to bring Gran home." Jesse's heart felt light as he drove Maddie's car to Las Cruces. One week to Easter. He could hardly wait to share this special season with her.

"I can't wait to see Emma again. I've missed her so much." Maddie sounded as eager to reunite with his grandmother as he felt.

Not that Emma hadn't kept in touch with them both. He and Maddie had shared his gran's pithy sayings and sage advice, which, though usually limited to emails or very short calls, were no less encouraging and appreciative of their efforts. Those glimpses had also shown Jesse the extent of Maddie's spiritual growth. Her direct questions to his gran revealed her ongoing struggle with letting go of past mistakes and feeling worthy, but also that she was growing in confidence in herself and her faith.

"Emma's emailed me at least twice a day since her surgery, but it's not the same as the heart-to-heart chats we've always had," he said thoughtfully. "I'm really looking forward to those."

"I hope she won't feel she has to get back to work right away." Maddie's smooth forehead pleated in a frown as she studied him. "Things are going smoothly at Quilt Essentials. I don't want her to rush her recovery."

"I think she'll be more than happy to leave it in your capable hands while she gets on with completing that to-do list of hers," Jesse told her, wondering if he should once again bring up the issue of Maddie buying Quilt Essentials. He knew his grandmother wanted that more now than she had before. If Maddie didn't buy, he had a sense Emma would put the business up for sale to someone else.

"I want to play Emma this song on my guitar. Listen, Jesse." Noah began strumming a haunting melody. The range tested his small fingers, but he kept going until the last note died away in eerie silence.

"That's really good, Noah. I bet your mom would like to hear it again later when the two of you are alone and there's no car noise." Jesse glanced at Maddie apologetically, trying to include her, but Noah merely grunted.

Jesse was having as little success reaching this kid as he was getting Kendal to explain the reason he kept acting up whenever the band met for practice. Though he'd thrown himself into the band, hoping to reach the kids with music, whatever ability he'd once possessed to communicate with youth seemed to have deserted him, making Jesse desperately yearn to get his gran's take on the situation. Maybe she could help him figure out exactly what he was doing wrong.

"We've arrived early. Emma won't be discharged till one. Why don't we stop for lunch?" he suggested.

"That sounds good." Maddie looked relieved. "We didn't have much breakfast this morning."

"Because it was burned." Noah's derisive tone matched the way he glared at his mother. "Never hurry when you're cooking. Dad's rule."

"I wouldn't have had to hurry so much if you hadn't spilled juice all over the kitchen floor," she murmured, then smiled as if to apologize. "But we made it and we're here in time so no big deal."

"It is so a big deal, because when you break the rules bad things happen," Noah sassed back. "Dad's rules—"

"How about if we declare today a rule-free day?" Jesse shot the boy a penetrating look meant to quell whatever criticism he was about to offer. "Let's enjoy this nice weather, each other and Gran's homecoming. Okay?" He kept a bead on Noah, trying to ensure that the kid understood he was serious about laying off these attacks on his mother.

"That's a good idea." Maddie pressed her back into the seat and cleared her throat. Jesse had a hunch she was in tears over Noah's crankiness, but he couldn't tell because of her sunglasses. "It was nice of you to have Emma's housekeeper come in to tidy up, Jesse, and I know she'll appreciate your thoughtfulness with the ramps. She'll certainly feel more secure with you there to call on if she has trouble."

"Well, I won't move in with her permanently, but I do want to make sure she's safe and capable of managing in her own home before I move back into my tent." He winked at her, just to watch the way she ducked her head in shy response. "And I'm doubly grateful you and Noah helped me get the last of the puppies to their new homes yesterday. The house seems empty without them, but we know they'll be well taken care of."

"It was hard to give them away. They were so cute." A smile of tenderness played across Maddie's pink lips. She was so lovely.

"We should have made sure the owners will

take good care of them." Noah wore his usual frown.

"How?" Maddie asked. Jesse guessed from her tone that she'd already had this discussion with her son.

"You should have given them my rule list," Noah snapped.

"That wouldn't be right," Jesse said quickly, before Maddie could reply. "The dogs have new owners who will each make their own rules. We've done our part." Then, because Noah still looked worried, he added, "But maybe we could phone them in a week or so and ask how the puppies are doing."

"And if they're not good?" Noah's question made it clear that he expected problems.

"Well, of course we can offer to help, but I'm sure they'll be fine." The boy's increasing worries and insistence on his rules were getting to Jesse. By now he'd hoped to alleviate at least some of Noah's concerns. Instead they seemed to be growing. "Is this a good place to have lunch?" He pulled into the parking lot of a national restaurant chain.

"Do they make good food?" The boy's wrinkled nose gave his opinion without saying a word. "Dad's rule was to eat at home."

"I'm sure it's very good food, Noah," Maddie

chided. "Jesse wouldn't have brought us here otherwise."

"I'll wash my hands really good. Do you know that if everyone washed their hands it would eliminate about a million deaths a year? Dad's rules—"

Jesse didn't hear the rest of it because he jumped out of the car, scooted around it, pulled open Maddie's door and held out his hand. "They have all-day breakfasts. I want waffles."

"With strawberries." She accepted his helping hand and didn't let go. "Thanks for driving. I know my car's a lot smaller than your truck, but I thought Emma might have trouble getting up on that high step."

"Studies show large trucks are the safest vehicles in an accident—"

"No talk about accidents today, okay, Noah? Let's talk about something pleasant. We don't want to spoil Emma's homecoming." Jesse grinned, but in his heart he was praying the kid would let go of his negativity and not spoil his time with Maddie. He looped her arm through his, laid his palm on Noah's back and ushered them both toward the restaurant. "I'm starving."

Once Noah returned from his hand-washing, the meal was a success. But that was only because Jesse refused to allow Noah's negativity to spoil it. When Maddie left for the ladies' room before their food was served, he asked Noah to stop nattering at her about his rules.

"Your mother loves you very much, Noah, but if I were her, I'd be getting pretty fed up with the way you're acting," Jesse told him in a no-nonsense voice.

"Me? Why?" Noah tried for an innocent look, but ducked his head when Jesse pinned him with a severe glance.

"You're deliberately being mean to her and I don't like it. I don't think your father would like it, either, if he were here," he said in a firm tone.

"He was mean to her all the time." Noah shredded part of his napkin.

"Does that make it right?" Jesse watched the kid struggle with the question. "I don't think so. It isn't the way God tells us to treat people we should love."

"He had to be mean 'cause she wouldn't follow his rules." Noah's tone was defiant. "It's important to follow Dad's rules."

"It's more important to follow God's rules and you're not doing that when you talk back to your mom and say mean things." Jesse didn't like to see Noah hurt, but how else to point out his mistake? And he was determined to do that. He would not sit back and watch Noah cause Maddie more distress. He couldn't stand to see her green eyes shadowed with heartache.

"I always follow Dad's rules." Noah's glare dared him to challenge that.

"Do you? Even if they're wrong?" There, he'd said it. "Anyway, I don't think you can follow any rules all the time. Sometimes I think you use your rules against other people to get your own way." Jesse felt like he was skating on thin ice, but he continued on. "I think you use your rules to force other people to do what you want. Your mom, me, even Kendal."

"How could I do that?" Noah scoffed.

"You didn't like it when I gave Kendal a solo for our Easter concert, did you? That's why you coax him to act out at band practice. You think that will make me angry and I'll take his solo part away." Jesse leaned forward. "Friends don't do that to friends, Noah. Because it's not keeping the rules that's most important. It's what's in your heart."

"My dad said keeping the rules is necessary." Noah's stubborn jaw lifted.

"How is that working for you, Noah? Are you able to keep all of them? Are you happy?" Jesse broke his stare only to smile at Maddie when she returned and sat down beside him. "Okay?"

"Perfect." Her eyes narrowed as she glanced from him to Noah. "What were you guys talking about?"

"Friends and how we treat them. Ah, here's our food." Jesse focused on helping Maddie enjoy their time together, surprised by how much her pleasure mattered to him.

He loved hearing her unbridled laughter, loved seeing the way she dabbed at her lips, trying to get all the maple syrup off. Loved the rub of her shoulder against his and the way she worked so hard to engage a recalcitrant Noah.

Jesse wanted to protect her, cherish her, erase the memories of the past and the harsh things Noah had hinted at. He wanted to spend hours with her discussing all the dreams she kept hidden inside. He wanted to know her secret hopes and fears. He wanted to help her teach Noah to embrace life and let go of his fear.

Jesse wanted a future with Maddie McGregor. But that was exactly what he didn't have to offer.

"Have all those carbs put you to sleep, Jesse?" she teased, nudging his side with her elbow.

"Nearly. I might have a sleep on the way home," he joked.

"While you're driving?" Noah looked and sounded aghast. "The rules—"

"Don't allow it. I know." Jesse winked at Maddie. "I was thinking your mom could drive."

She nodded. "I could. Let's go get Emma."

It was exactly what Jesse wanted to hear and he drove to the care center with a song in his heart, delighted to embrace his precious grandmother once more.

"I've missed you," Emma whispered in his ear as her arms tightened around him. It was the homecoming he'd longed for and Jesse reveled in it. She said the same to Maddie, hugging her tightly before commending her for the wonderful job she'd done at Quilt Essentials. "You're a great businesswoman, Madelyn McGregor. My bookkeeper says we've done better with you in charge than I ever managed."

"I'm sure that's not true," Maddie demurred. Though the sound of her formal name surprised him, it was easy for Jesse to see she was well pleased with the praise. "I hope everything is in order."

"I'm not worried in the least." Emma studied Noah for a moment before squeezing him close. "Noah, you've grown about two inches. How are you?"

"Good." He didn't exactly return her embrace, but he didn't wiggle away as Jesse had feared he would. "I'm sorry you got hurt," he said in his solemn voice.

"I'm much better now, thank you." Emma stood with the help of her walker and let her gaze roam over all three of them. "What are we waiting for? God's answered my prayers. Let's go home."

Maddie insisted on sitting in the backseat to give Emma room in the front, but trying to ensure she was comfortable wasn't easy, especially during Noah's steady stream of musical numbers. Her son didn't even pause in his guitar playing and ignored her soft-voiced requests for a break, but eventually fell into sullen silence when Jesse broke in to say he wanted to talk to Emma.

Mortified, Maddie shrank into her corner. What kind of a mother was she that she couldn't control her eight-year-old son? And why was Noah deliberately disobeying?

Eventually Emma fell asleep. Maddie was glad, even though it meant they didn't speak for the rest of the journey. Sometimes silence was better than trying to combat Noah's dark moods. Besides, she could spend the time admiring Jesse's good looks and the tender way he periodically glanced at his grandmother. She admired him so much.

Admired?

Who was she kidding? She loved him. Maddie squeezed her eyes closed and prayed desperately that God would make him love her, then returned to her senses and realized that was a foolish prayer. It would be absolutely right if He didn't answer that prayer, because Jesse was a pastor.

Oh, maybe not at this moment, but the way he worked with the kids at Wranglers Ranch told her he had a pastor's heart and sooner or later he would return to the work he'd been called to, work he loved. Work she couldn't share.

Hadn't Liam told her how useless she was in that regard? Hadn't she failed to be the leader the church ladies were supposed to find in their pastor's wife? Maddie had stopped going to their Bible studies because she'd never be able to offer insight on the Scriptures they studied, never felt she had anything to offer a hurting heart. She'd never given a talk on her faith or shared the sweet sorrows of other women or made a close friend of any of them. She certainly couldn't be the kind of helpmate that Jesse would need.

But she wanted to. Oh, how she wanted to be the woman who supported him through good times and bad. If only she could finally put her complete trust in God and truly believe that whatever path He led her on would be where He wanted her. If only God would let her be the one Jesse turned to.

It was a good thing Emma was back, Maddie

thought as they pulled into her driveway. Once her friend was settled, maybe she'd help Maddie understand how to accomplish the hardest part of the Bible study by finally letting go of the fear of love that her marriage to Liam had caused. Maybe then she could let herself be vulnerable to live and finally trust in God's love for her future.

If only Jesse could be part of that future.

Chapter Eleven

On Tuesday afternoon Maddie was up to her ears in Quilt Essentials' annual fabric sale when her phone rang.

"Could you go to Emma's? Now?"

She froze at the starkness of Jesse's voice. "Why?"

"Emma texted the word *help*. Something's wrong. I'll meet you there." There was a moment of silence, then he added, "And Maddie?"

"Yes?"

"Pray."

During the drive to Emma's Maddie begged God to remember that she wasn't asking help for herself, but for Emma, sweet wonderful Emma, and for Noah, who'd grown increasingly troubled and was spending more and more time with her. Maddie pulled up to the house a second before Jesse jumped out of his truck. He grabbed her hand and offered her a smile that calmed her. Jesse was here. They would handle this together.

Inside, they found Emma, her face contorted in a grimace, sprawled on the floor, with Noah kneeling beside her, his skin drained and sallow. Tears rolled down his cheeks as he muttered over and over, "It's my fault. You can't break the rules. That's why bad things happen."

Fear grabbed Maddie's heart. What had he done?

"Gran?" The tenderness in Jesse's voice and the way he carefully touched his grandmother's cheek made Maddie's heart swell. What a wonderful man he was.

"I'm fine, but I've twisted my ankle. Help me up, would you, please?"

With careful manipulation Jesse eased her upright, then lifted her in his arms and set her in her favorite armchair. Once seated, Emma turned to Noah.

"Honey, it's not your fault. It's mine."

"No." Noah's appearance echoed his ragged voice. "I broke the rule."

"What happened?" Jesse glanced from her to Noah and back.

"I didn't use my cane like I'm supposed to." Emma made a face. "So there was nothing to balance on when I tripped on the edge of the carpet. It's my own fault."

"Noah, you promised that if you could stay with Emma after school you'd help her." Maddie knew something was wrong because he wouldn't look at her. "Why didn't you bring her the cane?"

"I wasn't paying attention. I was playing my new song." The words emerged muffled because his chin was pressed against his chest. "I'm sorry, Emma." Noah hesitantly touched her hand, then backed up. "I wasn't playing a hymn. Dad said when you break the rules God makes bad things happen. He was right. Emma got hurt." He picked up his guitar and held it out. "I can't play this anymore."

Maddie lifted her head and stared straight at Jesse, hoping he had an answer. It was clear from his frowning face that he was as confused as she was.

"Playing songs that aren't hymns isn't breaking God's rules, Noah." Jesse's stare moved from the outstretched guitar to the boy's face. "Did you push Gran so she fell?"

Noah's head jerked and his eyes widened. "No!"

"Then how could it be your fault that she fell? She tripped. But she's all right now, aren't you, Gran?" Jesse smiled at her forceful nod.

"Yes. I thought I'd progressed past the wobbly stage, so I didn't use the cane. *I* broke the rule, Noah. Not you," she insisted.

Noah didn't look convinced as he returned the guitar to its case. He took a seat far away from it but his longing gaze kept returning to the instrument.

Maddie squelched a rush of frustration. Why couldn't she understand what was at the bottom of Noah's issues? Then Emma's pale face drew her attention.

"Would you like some tea?" Maddie hurriedly offered.

"I would love a strong cup of coffee," her boss said emphatically. "Would you make some, dear?"

"Of course." Maddie went to the kitchen and prepared a pot of coffee, her mind still on Noah. She smiled when Jesse appeared and sat at the breakfast bar.

"Any idea why he keeps on about breaking the rules?" he asked.

"No, but I'm beginning to believe he'll never get past that," she admitted, feeling she was failing her child. "I had reservations when Emma insisted he come here again today. Noah's been—I don't know. Not exactly acting out, but pushing against every restriction I make. His behaviour is getting stranger and I still feel that his coming here so often overtaxes your grandmother. She hasn't fully recovered."

"Emma's fine." Jesse frowned and scratched his chin. "Noah's issue is these rules your husband instilled in him. I think we need to stress that God wouldn't hurt Emma just because Noah broke a rule."

"It's kind of you, Jesse. I appreciate you taking an interest." She certainly did. "I have talked to him about the rules, but he doesn't seem to hear me. He's so angry at me and he won't say what it is that I've done wrong. He just keeps talking about the rules." Tears welled and there was no way she could stop them.

Suddenly Jesse's arms were around her. He gathered her against his chest, smoothing his hand down her back as he crooned words of comfort.

"You didn't do anything wrong, Maddie. No way. This is some crazy idea his father put in his head, or something Noah's twisted to understand." She felt Jesse's lips brush against her hair as he held her in the shelter of his embrace. "You've been sweet and loving to Noah, a truly caring mother. This isn't your fault."

Maddie stood silently absorbing the comfort as he stroked her back, encouraging her confidence.

"Dry your eyes and put on a happy face now,"

Jesse chided a few moments later. He held her at arm's length and smiled. "Or else Gran will know something is wrong and bawl me out for upsetting you."

Maddie sniffed and tried to nod. Then Jesse's hands cupped her face. She couldn't speak when he peered into her eyes. His own swirled with things she couldn't understand, while his thumbs grazed the skin of her cheeks, so lightly, so tenderly. She had a feeling he was struggling to decide something. Finally, he leaned forward and brushed his lips against hers in a brief touch that lit a fire in her heart and made it sing.

"You're so beautiful, Maddie. Such a precious heart you carry inside despite what you've been through. I don't think I've ever known anyone with a heart like yours." Then he kissed her again, and this time it was no mere brush of the lips. This time Jesse kissed her as if she was the person he prized most in the world.

Maddie gave herself to that kiss, trying to show him without words what he meant to her. She loved this man, loved him with all her heart. He was kissing her, so did that mean—

The creak of a floorboard made her draw back, breaking contact. She couldn't allow Noah to see them like this, so she turned away and busied herself setting out three mugs, which she filled with coffee. She picked up two and turned, leaving Jesse to carry his own.

"Emma says she could manage a cookie or two." Noah frowned. "You look funny."

"Do I?" She shook her hair off her face and scrounged up a smile. "I was worried about you and Emma, so I guess what you see is relief. But Noah, you—"

Jesse's hand on her arm stopped the rest of her words. He gave the merest shake of his head, then said, "There's juice in the fridge, Noah. Why don't you get some? You and I can have our coffee break in the backyard while your mom and Gran share theirs in the living room."

"Cookies?" he reminded them.

"I've got some for Emma. You and Jesse share the rest." Maddie wasn't sure what the former youth pastor could say to uncover her son's thoughts, but she hoped he'd fare better than she had, because Noah needed to talk about whatever burden he was carrying.

But when man and boy returned, Maddie knew from Jesse's face that he was still as much in the dark about Noah's rules as before. While Noah stowed his guitar in the car, Maddie paused on the doorstep beside Jesse.

"I'm sorry," he said.

"I know you tried," she murmured. "Thank you. I appreciate everything you've done for him. For us." She stepped back a little when he leaned forward. She couldn't afford to let Jesse hold her again lest she blurt out her feelings.

"Maddie," he said, frowning when he noticed her retreat. "About earlier—"

"Thank you for being our friend. We both appreciate you and Emma so much," she said as casually as she could, while forcing herself to walk toward the car, both loving and hating that he followed her. She wanted to be in his arms again. She pulled open her car door. "Don't forget we're decorating Wranglers Ranch on Good Friday afternoon. It's going to be a wonderful Easter."

"Easter always is." He nodded, though it was clear he had not said all he'd intended to. But Maddie drove off anyway. Jesse had kissed her as a man kisses a woman, but she couldn't tell if he'd meant it to be anything special.

And like the 'fraidy cat she was, she didn't want to ask. What if he told her no?

"Emma said I have to keep trusting You," she prayed as she drove. "And I'm trying to do that. But please put a bit of love for me in Jesse's heart, because I really, really love him."

The usual doubts assailed her later that night when she was alone, sitting on her deck and watching Mars appear in the night sky.

Why would Jesse care for her? Sure, he'd said

some nice things, but that's who Jesse was—a nice guy. She was a widow with a bad marriage behind her and a troubled child she couldn't seem to help.

What in the world would a man like Jesse see in Maddie McGregor?

On the afternoon of Good Friday Jesse tried hard to rein in the band as they practiced playing the final chorus of the Easter hymn he'd sung since he was a kid. And then, with a grin, he gave up and just listened.

"Make a joyful noise unto the Lord," the Bible said. This certainly qualified as noise. Who cared? Most of these kids had only recently learned to pluck out the melody of the hymn on their chosen instrument. Little things like tempo, loudness, timing—those didn't mean a thing to them. That they played at all was what mattered.

After the girl on the far end bashed her handbell in a grand finale, the last notes died away and the familiar sounds of horses and cattle at Wranglers Ranch returned.

"Amazing!" Maddie stood on the sidelines, eyes shining, clapping as hard as she could. "You guys are going to sound awesome on Easter morning."

Pride filled the kids' faces. Some of them half

bowed while others grinned, tucking their chins into their chests to hide their proud reactions.

"You did good, guys," Jesse affirmed, smothering the rush of love that took over his brain whenever he saw Maddie. "Remember to get here early on Sunday morning and to play with all your hearts, because Easter is above all a celebration."

He chatted with the kids as they packed up and left until only Noah remained, his guitar safely secured in its case.

"Did you enjoy playing today, Noah?" Jesse knew what the answer would be.

"I guess. If you're sure that's a hymn." The boy didn't look happy.

"You'll have to trust me." Jessie sighed. "I've studied the Bible a lot, Noah, and I never saw any passage that said making music was only okay if it was a hymn."

"Did they even have hymns in Bible days?" Maddie murmured.

"Not the same hymns we have now for sure," he said with a sideways look at Noah. He strummed a few notes on his own guitar, searching for a way to help, though it seemed that nothing he'd said thus far had made much difference. "Music is a way of expressing yourself. Sometimes happy, sometimes sad. Hymns are songs made up by somebody. They're nice, but you don't have to sing them, any more than the only way you can talk to God is by saying the Lord's Prayer. It's what's in our hearts that matters when we talk to God."

"But my dad said—"

"Your father did his best to teach you the right things, son." An urgency to help this child gripped Jesse. He hunkered down next to him. "But I think your father made mistakes. We all do. And I think one of his mistakes was about music."

"That's what you and Mom say, but how can *I* know the truth?" Noah whispered, his eyes stormy with confusion. "I have to know."

The same old quicksand of failure reached to grab Jesse. He wanted to leave, wanted to foist this off on somebody else. Let them give Noah advice. Let the consequences fall on their heads.

But there was no one else. Maddie had disappeared, as had Tanner, Lefty, Sophie and all the others. Right now Noah was looking to him for answers. How could Jesse fail this child?

Help me, Father, his soul begged in a silent plea.

And another voice seemed to answer. *I am the way, the truth and the life. No man comes to the Father but through me.*

"Noah, I don't have the answers you want," Jesse said as inspiration filled him. The boy's face fell, and he hurried to explain. "But I know who does."

"Who?" Noah waited, eyes wide.

"God. In 1 John 5, verse 15, it says that if we really believe that God is listening, when we talk to Him and ask Him what we need to know, He will answer us." Jesse crouched to Noah's level again so he could meet his stare head-on. "If you want to know what God thinks about this you need to ask Him."

"You think God is gonna talk to me?" Noah looked dubious.

"He talked to David and Samuel when they were kids. God speaks to our spirit and He can talk to anybody. You just have to listen with your heart." Jesse noted Lefty's urgent wave and rose. "I've got to get to work now, but try asking God about your rules."

"How?"

"Find a quiet place to pray and then be prepared to wait, and to listen for a whisper in your head and your heart. He'll let you know which rules are right."

Jesse hated to leave the kid but this was work and there were a hundred things to do to prepare for Wranglers' Easter Sunday service. As he walked away, he sent a heartfelt plea that God would use his words to help Noah but that feeble request didn't do much to assuage the lump of worry inside. Had he said the wrong thing again?

Jesse didn't want to even consider what his failure could cost Noah, and Maddie, too.

Chapter Twelve

"Doesn't Wranglers Ranch look fantastic?" Maddie twirled around, loving the festive decorations that were tucked here and there. "Beth's bunnies are perfect."

"I'm surprised she let you move them into that crate." Jesse's smile flicked up the corners of his lips.

He was such a handsome man, especially in his jeans and boots and that white Stetson. He always made her heart race when he shoved his hat to the back of his head, revealing his blue eyes.

"Tanner said his stepdaughter is very possessive about her bunnies."

"I promised they'd get carrot treats for their Easter breakfast." Maddie giggled when Jesse rolled his eyes. "It's almost time for the campfire sing-along," she said as she glanced around. "I haven't seen Noah for a while. Have you?"

"Not since we roasted our dinner." Jesse also surveyed the area.

"He only ate one hot dog and seemed pretty quiet." Maddie frowned as she scanned the ranch grounds. But she didn't see Noah anywhere.

"Maybe I'll go look for him," Jesse said.

"I'll go with you." She slid her hand into his, needing the comfort of his touch as worry feathered across her heart. "Noah usually sits on that log over there and plays on his tablet while he waits for me. But now that I think about it, though Tanner's kids were around while we were decorating, I didn't see Noah." Fear clamped a vise around her throat. "Where could he be?"

She felt Jesse tense and was about to ask his thoughts when Tanner appeared.

"Have you seen Noah?" she asked. "Is he with Davy and Beth?"

"No. Sophie took the two of them in to bathe. They're allowed to be at the campfire for a little while before they get tucked in." He frowned. "Where have you looked?"

Jesse told him, because Maddie couldn't say anything. Fear filled her, growing by the moment as a voice she thought she'd finally silenced began to repeat her failures.

How could you lose your son, Madelyn? Noah's a child. He can't manage on his own. You're his mother. You're supposed to be the responsible one, but as usual you've failed. Nothing's changed. You're as incompetent as ever. You should never have had a child, never have been a mother. You're unworthy of that trust.

She gulped, tears welling. She'd tried so hard to have faith, to believe God cared about her. But if He did, then why—

"Don't look like that, Maddie," Jesse begged. "Noah's fine. He's probably playing a game, hiding someplace and trying to fool us."

"Maybe." She knew it wasn't true. Noah didn't play games. Ever.

"I'll organize the hands. We'll do a search of the ranch. Does he have his backpack?" Tanner's face tightened when Maddie told him it was on the backseat of her car. "We'll find him. Just keep praying."

"I should have been watching him more closely," Maddie whispered, her heart squeezing at the thought of what could happen. "Instead I got so caught up in decorating Wranglers, in preparing for Easter—" She shoved her fist into her mouth to choke back her tears.

"Maddie's, it's going to be okay." Jesse

hugged her close. But although Maddie desperately wanted to believe him, fear had crept in and held her heart captive.

"You don't know that," she whispered. "The days have warmed with spring. There's a lot more talk of rattlers coming out. There have been sightings of cougars, even coyotes. If something happened…" She couldn't give voice to it. "It's my fault. I haven't been the mother Noah needed. I should have—"

"Stop it, Maddie." Jesse's hands tightened on her shoulders. She lifted her gaze to meet his and forced herself to listen. "Noah will be fine. God is with him. He will protect your boy until we can find him. But you have to trust Him. Okay?"

"I'll try," she whispered, trying but failing to return the smile he gave her.

"You have to do more than try," he pleaded, his eyes dark and serious. "Now, right now, is the time to show God you trust Him. No doubts, no fears. Push them all away. You are a beloved child of God. He is your father, a father who cares for you so much He sent His beloved son for you. He made you and He has great things in store for your future."

Maddie stared at Jesse, loving the way he spoke, so calm, so certain. Then he took her hands in his. His voice dropped as he said words meant for her ears alone.

"I've seen how wonderful a mother you are. You'd give anything for Noah. God knows how much you love your child because that's exactly how He feels about you. He sees every tear you shed, hears every prayer you pray. God loves you, Maddie, and He is going to bring Noah back safe and sound. Don't let go of that, okay?" Jesse waited a moment for her nod, pressed a kiss into her palm and closed her fingers around it.

In his arms Maddie felt safe, free from her constant self-doubt, whole. With Jesse trust was simple.

"I have to go look for Noah now, Maddie." He hugged her close, then pulled back to stare into her eyes. "Will you trust God?"

That's when she understood. Trust was a decision. Trust wasn't something that fell on you like manna had fallen for the Israelites. Trust was a verb, an action.

"I will trust," she whispered.

Jesse leaned closer to hear, so she said it again, this time a little louder. A big smile stretched across his face. He bent forward, pressed his lips to hers, then drew back.

"Keep that up, daughter of God," he said.

After a long look that made Maddie feel confused and oddly shy, he hurried away.

"Daughter of God," she mused, when he'd disappeared. She needed to think about that. "That would make Noah God's grandson."

And what grandfather wouldn't want his grandson returned to the home where he was loved?

Maddie's phone rang.

"Jesse explained. I'm in a taxi on my way to Wranglers Ranch," Emma said. She cut through Maddie's protests. "I'll be there in twenty minutes. They'll find him, sweetie. Noah is going to be just fine. 'The Lord your God is God, the faithful God. He will keep His agreement of love for a thousand lifetimes.' Remember that, honey."

"I'm trusting God," Maddie told her. A burst of confidence began to seep into her heart as she walked toward the house.

God loved her. Trusting would get easier, but she'd have to practice. She would practice with Emma, because her friend always knew the right words to say to God. Right now Maddie could only repeat, "I'm trusting You."

He couldn't watch Maddie's face when Tanner told her they hadn't found Noah.

Jesse veered his horse away from the other

searchers while his heart begged God to direct him to Noah. He rode away from the house on the track where he'd helped with so many lessons, away from where the other hands were unsaddling their horses. He was as weary as they after a fruitless night of searching, and yet he was still plagued by that unanswerable question. Why?

It wasn't yet dawn. He dismounted under a sprawling eucalyptus tree, chilled from the bitter wind blowing off the mountains and across the desert floor. Noah was out in this, without his jacket, alone, hungry and thirsty, and probably terrified because his rules weren't working. Bleak despair fought a battle for Jesse's mind.

Why? Why hadn't God shown them where the boy was, given them a sign to follow, something? Why couldn't they have found him and brought him back to his worried mother? Why would God want Maddie to go through the torture of not knowing where her child was?

It was always why, ever since Scott had died. And still Jesse had no answer.

Frustrated, he tied his mount to a fence rail and sat down on top of a massive rock. There had to be something, some clue that would tell him where the boy had gone. He closed his eyes and tried to think of what had happened when he'd last seen Noah.

And then Jesse caught his breath. His eyes blinked open as horror filled his heart and soul.

"Find a quiet place to pray and then be prepared to listen for a whisper in your head and in your heart. He'll let you know which rules are right."

A quiet place. Had Noah interpreted a quiet place as somewhere away from the hubbub of activity on Wranglers Ranch? Had he gone into the desert alone?

"I'm begging you God," Jesse pleaded aloud, his heart aching at the horror of reliving another mistake. "Don't let this child be lost because of me. Not again."

"Jesse?" Maddie stood staring at him, her face confused. "I was looking for you. What do you mean? How could it be your fault that Noah's missing?"

"I—I might have said something, Maddie." He wanted to beg her to understand, but there wasn't time. It would be sunrise soon. Noah had been alone all night, perhaps suffering from hypothermia by now. So Jesse repeated what he'd said to Noah.

"Yes, but…" He could tell she didn't understand.

"Don't you see? It's my fault he's missing. It's just more proof that I shouldn't be in the ministry. I've made another mistake and this time

I'm not sure…" He couldn't go on, couldn't say the unthinkable.

"Oh, Jesse." Maddie's arms went around him as she hugged him close. "You're as wrong as Noah is. God isn't punishing you. Remember what you told me? We're His beloved children."

"Yes, but—" He stopped, because she laid her forefinger over his lips and shook her head.

"We don't know God's ways. Even if we did I doubt we'd understand. But we do know that everything God does is for a purpose." Her soft smile begged him to hear her words. "I don't know why Noah's missing, Jesse. But I do know that God is watching over him, caring for him, because you taught me that's what a loving father does."

Maddie's face shone. Her green eyes glowed with inner peace as she pushed a hank of hair out of his eyes and grazed his cheeks with her fingers.

"I'm Noah's mother and I love him dearly, but God loves Noah way more than I ever could. He cares like that for you, too. It wasn't a horrible tragedy that brought you to Wranglers Ranch, Jesse. It was God. He has a reason and I believe it was so you could help Noah. And you have."

Tears welled in her lovely eyes as she gazed at him. Tears and something else, something Jesse was afraid to believe he was seeing, something he was afraid to trust again—love?

"Before you came Noah was so reclusive. He shut out the world, would hardly speak to anyone, let alone interact. Everything had to fit into his rigid rules." She held his face between her palms. "I'd almost given up on him changing. Until you." Her smile made his heart gallop. "You refused to let Noah keep his walls up. You kept breaking through them, forcing him to see the world and to see good. I will never forget you did that, Jesse."

"But Noah's missing," he said, when he could get his voice back.

"Yes." She nodded. "And I don't know why. I only know that if God is God in my life, I have to let Him be in charge right now." She pushed Jesse's Stetson off his head and ran her fingers through his hair. "Children can't always understand why their parents do what they do. Neither can we always understand our Father's ways. But God's in control, Jesse. He *will* do what is best for my son."

The calm way she spoke, the peace in her green eyes, the gentle way she touched him—all of these told Jesse that Maddie had undergone a spiritual transformation.

"You prayed and asked God to work in your ministry and He has. Tanner told me that you touched the lives of a lot of kids in Colorado. And then God led you here, because He works all things together for those who love Him," she reminded him. "Even bad things, things we don't like, things we don't understand. So either we trust Him or we fuss and complain and fight to understand. And stay frustrated."

"How did you get to be so smart?" Jesse wove his arms around her narrow waist, loving the way her lips curved up in that Maddie smile that no one else could copy.

"I had your grandmother as my coach," she said with a wink. "But think about it. What if God asked you to stay at Wranglers Ranch? Could you live with that, do your best and trust God to make it work?"

As Jesse stood holding Maddie in his arms, truth dawned, a truth he hadn't been willing to accept before now.

Be still and know that I am God.

God didn't owe him any answers. He was God. That had to be enough. Either Jesse trusted Him and did whatever work he was sent, or he kept trying to understand what wasn't his to comprehend. In sudden clarity he realized that if he hadn't been forced to leave Colorado he'd never have come to Tucson, would never have met Maddie, never felt this heart-pounding reaction to her.

Never known what real love was.

Whatever you do, work at it with all your heart, as working for the Lord, not for human masters.

Time to get to work for the Lord and leave the results to God.

"You are a very wise woman, Maddie McGregor. And I love you." He kissed her squarely on the lips, not caring a hoot if Tanner or Lefty or even Gran was watching them. "Your heart is pure and honest, and you see God as I haven't been seeing Him for a long time. I know it seems soon. I know I should have led up to this, done things differently. But I didn't. That doesn't change the fact that I love you."

"That's good," she said demurely, fiddling with his collar before she looked at him from between her lashes. "Because I love you, too. I didn't want to. Romance never turned out the way I expected so I thought I'd just shut love out of my world. But I don't want to shut you out. You're what makes my world fun and interesting and happy. I love you, Jesse."

They shared a sweet kiss that didn't last nearly long enough but soothed the hearts of both, for now. Then Jesse drew back and bowed his head.

"God, thank You for Maddie and her love. I don't know why she loves me, but I don't have to. I'll gladly take whatever You give me." He opened his eyes to smile at her. "But now will You please help us find Noah? Because we love him and we need him with us to make our family complete. Thank You for caring for him and for us. Amen."

"Amen," Maddie whispered in a teary voice, but her smile was happy. She held out her hand. "Let's go find him, Jesse."

They'd gone about two feet when Jesse heard a noise.

"Listen," he whispered. "Someone's in that old shed. Crying."

"It's Noah." Maddie hurried forward and yanked on the weathered door, which creaked open. "Honey, are you in here?"

"Go 'way."

"We can't do that. We've been looking all over for you," Jesse said. "Your mom and I have been really worried."

"Why?" Noah sniffed. "You tol' me to find a quiet place and ask God about the rules." Tears were rolling down his cheeks. "I listened and listened but I can't hear nothing."

"Oh, sweetheart." Maddie surged forward and wrapped her arms around him. "I love you, Noah. I don't ever want you to hide out like this again. Everybody's been looking for you," she said, after she'd kissed his forehead.

Noah pulled away from her, but only a little.

"Looking...why?" he asked, his brows drawn together.

"Because you've been gone all night and we couldn't find you."

"All night?" Noah seemed confused. "Did I sleep through Easter?"

"No, honey. Easter is tomorrow. But we were very worried." Maddie fixed her gaze on her son. "Why did you come in here, Noah? What's been troubling you?" When he didn't answer, she leaned closer to brush a kiss against his cheek. "Jesse and I love you. So does Emma. We care that you haven't been happy. Can you tell us why?"

"I can't keep Dad's rules." Noah burst into tears again, his agitation growing. "I tried really hard, Mom, but I can't do it."

"But Noah, we've tried to tell you that you don't have to keep all your father's rules." Maddie looked to Jesse for confirmation, and he was ready.

He knew now that Noah was the reason he'd been sent here. There was something God needed him to help this child understand. Jesse had been called to be a pastor and it was about time he did his job and helped this child find the answer he craved.

"Why do you have to keep all your dad's

rules, Noah?" Jesse kept his voice low, but every sense was on high alert. He slid his hand into Maddie's, loving that she was whispering a prayer for them all.

"'Cause I promised." Noah sniffed.

"Promised whom?" Maddie glanced from him to Jesse, then lifted her shoulders to show her lack of understanding.

Noah's face tightened and his dark eyes started to get that blank look. In that moment Jesse knew.

"You promised your dad, right?" The boy nodded. "When did you promise him, Noah?"

"The day he died. It was my fault he died," Noah wailed.

"Honey, no. You weren't even there."

"Yes, I was, Mom. I got home from school early. I was waiting for you and I got hungry. So I hid behind that big hanging that was at the front of the church and ate an orange I had left in my lunch. But I got some of it on the hanging." His face was a picture of misery and shame. "I tried to wash it off but it got worse, and Dad saw me. I broke his rules about not eating in the church and he was so mad. He was yelling at me and then his face got a funny look. I was really scared when he sat down on the chair, like he couldn't stand up."

Jesse glanced at Maddie, who was staring at Noah as if she'd never seen him before.

"And then what happened?" he coaxed gently, while Noah sobbed as if his heart would break.

"Dad said really loud, 'Bad things happen when you break the rules. Obey.' Then he flopped over, like this." The boy slumped face-down to demonstrate. "I shook his arm 'cause I thought he was sleeping," he whispered, his voice breaking. "Th-that's what made him fall off the chair and die. I killed Dad when I broke the rules."

Noah wept uncontrollably. Maddie blinked, her mouth working as if searching for the right thing to say to console her son. Jesse took her hand and squeezed it. And when she glanced at him he shook his head, knowing Noah needed to say it all, to get his secret completely out in the open. It had been festering in him for too long.

"I tried and tried to keep his rules, but I can't. There are too many. I keep making mistakes. I'm sorry, Mom. I'm really sorry." Noah threw himself into her arms, holding tight.

"You were mad at your mom because she said it wasn't important to keep your dad's rules, is that right?" Jesse nodded at Maddie's surprised look.

"Yeah." Noah pulled away. "I *gotta* keep his rules, Mom. I promised."

Finally. Jesse couldn't smother his grin, even though Maddie frowned at him. He leaned over to brush his lips against hers, knowing beyond a shadow of a doubt what he needed to do.

He was a pastor, would always be a pastor for as long as God needed him. This was what he was created to do. Jesse inhaled, sent a silent thank-you heavenward, then got about His Father's business.

"Listen to me, Noah." He smiled at Maddie to reassure her then continued. "The Bible says man looks at the outward things, but God looks at your heart. That means all the rule-keeping in the world won't help you one bit if you don't have love in your heart. That's what God cares about. When you have His love, you don't need to worry about all the rules, because inside, in your heart, you'll want to do the things that please God and He'll help you keep His rules."

Noah looked confused. Jesse's heart ached for him. How he cared for this child, wanted him to be free of his guilt. How he wanted to help Noah find freedom and joy and happiness in life.

He stared at Maddie. Their precious time together would come, but for tonight he needed to focus on her son.

"I know tomorrow's Easter," he whispered

in her ear. "And you and I have some talking to do. But I was wondering if it would be okay if Noah and I camped out in my tent tonight. I think it's going to take some one-on-one time to help him let go of the rules."

Maddie's glorious smile flashed across her face even though her lovely green eyes brimmed with tears. She lifted her hand to cup his cheek.

"One more reason why I love you, Jesse Parker," she said softly. "And yes, I think Noah would love to go camping with you."

"Did you say camping? With me? Well, did you?" Impatient when neither his mother nor Jesse responded immediately, Noah repeated the question, then danced for joy at their response. "I'm going to tell the others. I'm going camping!"

"I love you, Jesse."

"I love you, Maddie."

Chapter Thirteen

It wasn't even 6:00 a.m. but Maddie couldn't sleep.

She pulled on her cotton housecoat and slippers, then padded to the kitchen to make coffee, unable to suppress her smile.

Thank You, God, her heart sang. *Thank You for Easter, thank You for Your love and thank You for Jesse.*

She stepped outside onto her deck and froze, surprised to see the love of her life already seated on her porch swing.

"Happy Easter." Jesse rose, wrapped her in his arms and kissed her, then pressed her into the swing and knelt in front of her.

"My darling Maddie," he said softly, as the first faint rays of sunrise peeked over the craggy mountaintops. "God put you into my life because He knew you are the perfect woman for me. I love you. I want to marry you. Not today, not even tomorrow. First I want to court you, get to know you and Noah better, maybe wait till you finish cooking class—"

"Jesse!" she giggled.

"But when the time is right for us, will you marry me, Maddie?"

"Yes," she whispered, her heart aching. "Because I love you. You build me up and encourage me and make me stronger. Together we are whole. We can trust God with our futures because He works all things together for good. When the time is right, I'll marry you, Jesse."

Jesse rose and pulled her into his embrace. They exchanged kisses in a silent promise to cherish each other.

"You guys are missing the sunrise," Noah chided. He flopped down on the deck, one arm around Cocoa's neck, his guitar case at his feet as he studied the peach-toned sky flaming across the desert.

"Not a chance." Maddie pulled Jesse to sit beside her on the porch swing and savor God's latest masterpiece.

"Happy Easter!" A grin splashed across Noah's face. "Want to hear my new song?"

"Yes," they said together, then laughed for the pure joy of it.

"What's your song about, son?" Maddie asked, keeping her hand tucked inside Jesse's.

"Love." Noah plucked a few strings on his guitar. "I'm going to sing it at your wedding."

"You mean at the band concert today?" Jesse asked, glancing at Maddie.

"Uh-uh. That's Kendal's solo. This one's for your wedding."

"And you're okay with us getting married, being a family?" Maddie glanced at Jesse and felt the comfort of his reassuring smile.

"Sure." Noah nodded.

"How come?" Clinging to Maddie's hand Jesse leaned back, waiting to see if his talk had done any good.

"Well, God brought you here 'cause He knew we needed you," Noah explained. "I needed you to help me understand that keeping God's rules is what matters."

"Right." Jesse squeezed Maddie's hand while they waited for Noah to continue.

"And Mom needed you to help her not feel so bad about her cooking," Noah explained in his most serious tone. "We need you to love us and you need us to love you. 'Cause God is all about love."

"You are so right, son." Maddie told herself not to cry.

"I'm glad God sent you for another reason, too, Jesse."

"Really?" Maddie smiled. Noah's flattery was making her beloved's chest inflate. "What reason is that?"

"'Cause He knew I needed someone to show me how to make s'mores and go camping and roast hot dogs." Noah's grin made them both laugh. "I think we're gonna make a good family. I figure that as long as I make sure I have love in my heart He'll make sure you and Mom do, too."

"You're a very smart boy, son." Maddie kissed the top of his head and proudly grinned at Jesse.

"Like mother, like son," he quipped.

"You've always loved Easter, Jesse." Emma smiled as he helped her into a chair beside Maddie at Wranglers Ranch, ready to share in the Easter service.

"Always," he agreed.

"I have a hunch you're going to enjoy this one best of all." Emma struggled to keep her expression blasé.

"This is the beginning of many happy Easters, Gran." He hugged her tight, so thankful she'd been praying for him his entire life.

"I gather this means you've figured out God's leading and don't require my help?" Emma's soft chuckle as she glanced from him to Maddie and back said that, as usual, she understood.

"Maddie and I will always want your help," he assured her.

"I should hope so since I'm the one who brought you together," she said with a wink. "Only took a little time in hospital for the two of you to figure out what I've known for ages. That's why I've been praying God would lead you here."

"You—" Jesse caught Tanner's eye and knew he had to leave. "We'll talk about this later." He wasted a few more minutes gawking at Maddie, still not quite believing this wonderful woman had promised to marry him.

"They need you now, Jesse. It's going to be wonderful." Her smile sent his heart racing. "I'll be praying."

Dazed with happiness he walked to the front while marveling at their creator. God loved mankind enough to send His only son. That was the true message of Easter. And that love was what had grounded him through the most difficult time in his life.

That love had given him Maddie.

Jesse turned, searched until he found her smiling face among the group and basked in the peace he saw there. Then he faced his band.

"Ready?" he asked sotto voce. They looked

so scared. He tapped his baton on the music stand and asked again, "Ready?"

No one spoke. Was this all for naught?

Trust.

"Ready," Noah called out.

A second later every band member responded.

"Good. Now remember, this is the day that the Lord has made. We will rejoice."

Knowing Maddie would be praying through the entire concert, Jesse lifted his hand and led his students in playing the Hallelujah chorus. Deep satisfaction filled him.

Wranglers Ranch was where he belonged.

With Maddie and Noah, and any other children God sent his way.

Epilogue

At five o'clock on the longest day in June, Maddie walked down the aisle of her church on Noah's arm. Jesse felt confident and secure in the knowledge that the woman who was walking toward him loved him as much as he loved her. Today their Easter family wish would come true.

After Noah placed Maddie's hand in Jesse's he stepped to one side, lifted his guitar and began to sing the beautiful song he'd first played for them on Easter morning, a song of God's grace and love, of understanding and forgiveness and, of course, of joy.

Amid the sweet, poignant silence of its ending Noah took his seat beside Emma, whom he now also called Gran, grinning as she hugged him close.

"Noah, the rings," Maddie reminded him in a whisper.

Noah gave the bride and groom a broad wink then put his fingers to his lips. A shrill whistle filled the sanctuary.

Gasps turned to laughter as Cocoa stepped smartly down the aisle bearing a white satin pillow with two rings tied on top. She stopped in front of the bridal couple just long enough for them to remove their rings, then raced over to sit by Noah.

He hugged her tightly, then announced, "I taught Cocoa to do that, Jesse. She's part of our family, too, so she had to be part of the wedding."

Laughter finally died away when the minister cleared his throat. And then, with the past settled and the future waiting, he and Maddie made their promises of love to each other.

"Jesse, every day you show me what real love is. You encourage and support me to be the best I can be. I am blessed to be loved by you." Maddie slid the ring on his finger, then touched her lips to it. "I promise I will always be there supporting you in whatever God gives us to do. I love you."

"Maddie, you are the most beautiful woman I've ever known." Jesse cupped her scarred face in his hand and stared into her eyes. "Your heart shines with the love that you give so freely. I had no idea that God would bless me so much when He led me to Tucson and you. I will spend the rest of my life loving you and Noah. Together we'll trust Him to lead and guide every step along our life's journey. I love you, Maddie." He slid a slim gold band onto her finger next to a shiny solitaire he'd bought the day after Easter.

"Having exchanged their vows before God and these witnesses, and pledging their commitment each to the other, I now pronounce that they are husband and wife. You may kiss the bride!"

As the couple sealed their promise with a kiss, their guests applauded. Jesse knew Noah waited as long as he could, but apparently he felt they'd never stop kissing because he strode forward and tugged on Jesse's pant leg to get his attention.

"Isn't it time to go to Wranglers Ranch for the party?"

Jesse smiled at Maddie and wondered when they'd get a few minutes alone. "What's the rush?"

Noah motioned for him to bend down. "Sophie said the food is gonna be in triangles. *All* of it," he emphasized, his eyes huge.

"Really?" Jesse tried to look suitably impressed. "And you love triangles, I know."

"I like triangles," Noah corrected. He smiled at his mom. "I like triangles a lot. But I love God. And you guys, and Gran, and Cocoa, and…"

"Our brilliant son sure has his priorities figured out." Jesse looped his bride's arm through his. "Lead on to the party, Noah."

Smiling, he and Maddie followed Noah down the aisle and out of the church, to where Lefty waited by a horse-drawn carriage.

"And that's not all." Noah fed Amos a sugar lump, waiting as Jesse helped his bride into the decorated carriage. When he whistled for Cocoa to jump in, too, lifted Noah inside and followed himself, Noah continued. "Me and the band are gonna play a special song."

"Really?" Jesse grinned in delight.

Noah's face drooped. "Oops. That was supposed to be a secret."

"I didn't hear anything. Jesse, did you?" It seemed Maddie couldn't stop smiling at him and Jesse didn't mind that one bit.

"They're kissing again," he heard Noah mumble before turning his face forward.

"Reckon you better get used to it, son, 'cause I'm thinking there's gonna be a whole lot of that in your future," Lefty chuckled, picking up the reins.

"I know," Noah replied, as the horse clopped down the street toward Wranglers Ranch.

Delighted by his acceptance, Jesse hugged Maddie and whispered, "This is the start of our future, Mrs. Parker."

"You'll be helping kids just like God told you so long ago."

"And Noah will want to go camping with me at least once a month," Jesse predicted in a louder voice, shooting the boy a grin. "While my wife will be running Quilt Essentials with Gran and taking care of everybody who touches that sweet heart of hers."

Her cream Stetson dipped demurely.

"In between caring for my family," she reminded him.

That sounded absolutely perfect to Jesse.

"I love knowing that God's in charge, don't you, Maddie?"

"Yes." Maddie winked at Noah, then motioned for him to turn around.

Their precious son pretended he didn't see a thing as Jesse's wife told him exactly how she felt without using a single word.

* * * * *

If you enjoyed this story,
pick up the first two
WRANGLERS RANCH *books,*
THE RANCHER'S FAMILY WISH
HER CHRISTMAS FAMILY WISH
and these other stories from Lois Richer:

A DAD FOR HER TWINS
RANCHER DADDY
GIFT-WRAPPED FAMILY
ACCIDENTAL DAD

Available now from Love Inspired!

Find more great reads
at www.LoveInspired.com

Dear Reader,

Welcome back to Wranglers Ranch where you're always welcome.

Isn't self-confidence hard? Maddie had to learn that as God's creation she was worthy of being loved and could love without fear.

Poor Jesse got caught in the whirlpool of *why?* But when we realize that God doesn't owe us an explanation, we can rest knowing He has everything under control.

I'd love to hear from you. You can reach me at: loisricher@gmail.com; www.loisricher.com; on Facebook: loisricherauthor or via snail mail at:

Lois Richer, Box 639, Nipawin, Sask., Canada S0E 1E0

Till we meet again I wish you the confidence of knowing that God loves you dearly, the peace of not needing answers to your *why*s and the joy of knowing Him who is able to do exceedingly, abundantly above all that we could ask or think.

Blessings,

Lois Richer